MY FAVE THING

HAJI SM

World Castle Publishing, LLC
Pensacola, Florida
Copyright © 2023 Haji SM
Hardback ISBN: 9798864325407
Paperback ISBN: 9798891260801
eBook ISBN: 9798891260818
First Edition World Castle Publishing, LLC, October 23, 2023
http://www.worldcastlepublishing.com

Licensing Notes

Cover: Cover Designs by Karen
Editor: Karen Fuller

Table of Contents

PROLOGUE
THE RHYTHMIC KNOCKING

Once upon a time, not so long ago, a great snowstorm blew across Ireland, burying everything under a giant blanket of snow.

The wind howled menacingly, like a banshee with a headache, shaking the roof tops and windowpanes with its chilling claws. The seas turned grey and wild, causing even the hardy seagulls to stay silent in their nests.

Of course, the children thought this was all great fun at first. Snowmen popped up everywhere, and the frosty air rang with shouts and laughter from snowball fights and sled rides.

But the storm never stopped raging. The days stretched into weeks, weeks into months. The pale sun, on the rare occasions, peeked out meekly behind dark thunder clouds.

People started to grow hungry. All the fruit and

vegetables withered under the frost. Without crops, there was nothing to feed the animals. The cows, pigs, sheep, and the chickens tumbled down where they stood. The butchers, bakers, and greengrocers all locked up their doors, for they had nothing worthy left to sell.

Safe to say, things were not so much fun anymore.

People of faith prayed in their homes, for the great storm forced many away from the holy places. Thus, the great halls of worship, in all their assorted shapes and sizes, became as quiet as graves.

The worst to suffer were the children. Such was the way of the world, the younger you were, the hungrier you got. Hence, hungry and miserable, the children also prayed in their own special way. In order to avoid starving, people began rationing. Food of all kinds, from fresh to frozen, salted to smoked, anything at all that could be eaten was rationed.

One food was prized above all else, and that was the humble bread, or more precisely, the flour which people used to make them. Even if everything else ran out, as long as there was some flour left, life was still bearable. Hence, everyone guarded their stock of flour jealously, like dragons hoarding their gold. In time, those who were able to make and sell flour were considered amongst the richest and most important in the land.

It was during these dark times that the knockings started on people's doors and windows, believed to be by fey beings that came with the freezing mist in the dark of night. No definite sightings were ever made as people were too fearful to peek out.

But things turned horribly wrong, as children and pets began vanishing from their homes, never to be seen again. People came to dread that awful sound, the rhythmic knocking, which we will come to a bit later…

Knock…

Knock…

Knock…

CHAPTER 1
A SOFT TAPPING

Mary gasped as her eyes snapped open, the nightmare still gnawing fresh in her brain. She lay in bed, shivering beneath her thin blanket, the cold midnight air seeping through the windowpanes.

Her eyes slowly adjusted to the pitch dark, her pounding heart slowing as the shadows retreated to the corners of her bedroom. The harsh whispers of a gale filled her ears, but this was something she was used to.

There it was again, a soft tapping sound that had penetrated her slumber.

It must be those rats again, playing behind the walls, thought Mary.

On instinct, she ran her fingers across her delicate lips. Still intact. Mary breathed a sigh of relief. She overheard her Mam once saying that hungry rats like to creep into babies' cots and chew on their lips and eyelids.

She tried hard to recall her latest nightmare, of a man with a long beard and the whiff of an awful smell, but it was fading fast behind a wall in her memories.

Tap...

Tap...

Tap...

Mary's heart froze with fear. The sound was coming from the window. She suppressed an overwhelming desire to dash for her Mam's room.

"C'mon, girl," whispered Mary to herself. *"You're ten! Double digits mean you have to be brave. And Mam's so tired, she needs her sleep..."*

Mary thought of her Mam sleeping with her baby brother next door. Her Mam's back pain was flaring up, and Tom was being very restless, crying late into the night. Mam said babies were very sensitive. They could sense things that adults were blind to.

Tap...

Tap...

Tap...

I hope it's not the thing Tom was sensing, thought Mary fearfully, her heart beating hard against her chest. There had been rumors of missing children taken from their homes, right under their parents' very noses.

Mary never knew her father, and she never asked

about him. Her Mam had raised her, cared for her, and that was enough. She also had Tom, her baby brother, whom she adored. Now that her Mam's back was sore, Mary must step up and be more responsible.

Mary sat up, her brown eyes fixed on the curtained window. *Was that a shadow of someone's head peeking in?*

Tap…

Tap…

Tap…

Slowly, Mary slid her skinny legs from beneath the blanket over the side of her bed, already counting how many steps she needed to reach the door and out into safety, her breaths rapid with fear. Her left foot touched the cold floorboards.

"Aagghh…!"

Something furry with sharp claws ran across her toes. Mary had to bite her tongue to stifle a scream, tasting blood at the back of her throat. She looked down in time to see a thin rat's tail disappearing under the cupboard.

Double digits, girl! she scolded herself. *It's just a silly rat! Mam and Tom need you to be brave and not jump at every little thing!* Mary turned to get back into bed.

Tap…

Tap…

Tap…

Mary froze. Icy prickles of fear ran down her neck. She now knew for certain something was lurking behind her window; she sensed a dark menace just a few feet from where she was standing.

But how could it be? It was a sheer drop of three stories to the concrete pavement below. Her Mam would not want to be disturbed if there was a logical explanation for this. She needed to find out.

Double digits, be brave...

Maybe she was sleepwalking, and this was all in her mind?

Mary took a deep breath and stepped closer to the window. She reached out a trembling hand and slowly pulled back the curtain.

It was all black.

Outside her window, there were no stars, no lights from the streets, just a solid wall of impenetrable darkness. Mary let out her breath in relief. She could just make out her reflection in the glass, her pale face staring back at her.

There now, just your brain going overdrive again. Nothing to be scared of...

Mary blinked and stared at her reflection, a sudden chill shooting down her spine. Her reflection was grinning grotesquely in the dark glass, showing delicate, sharp fangs, its black eye pits boring into her. It reached up and, with a clawed finger, tapped on the other side.

Tap…

Tap…

Tap…

Mary stood frozen in horror, beads of cold sweat forming on her upper lip. The entity shrieked in a voice from her nightmares, not of a ten-year-old girl but of an old man, hoarse and wheezy.

"Let me in! Let me in!"

Mary stepped back from the window, her image leering at her with malevolent eyes, hammering the other side of the glass with its fists.

"Let me in! You silly girl!"

The creature's face melted like gooey candle wax, reshaping, as Mary stared in horrid fascination, into that of a hideous beast with a long snout and a maw with dagger-sharp fangs.

It leered at her hungrily, its piggy eyes hypnotizing her in an icy grip.

Mary felt all her will dissolve away, just how a mouse must have felt when trapped under the paw of a hungry cat.

BANG!

BANG!

BANG!

The incessant pounding reverberated around her tiny bedroom as the creature continued pummelling the glass in a berserker's fury.

A large crack suddenly appeared in the window. An awful stench blasted Mary's senses, the nauseating odor of a long-dead animal momentarily clearing her head. She saw the beast drawing its arm back a final time, then punching through, the myriads of shattered glass cutting her delicate face and arms.

"I'm the Beastie, little Mary! I'll eat your heart out!"

The creature pushed its large head through in a frenzy, drawn by the sweet smell of Mary's blood, its fanged maw gnashing wildly.

Mary turned for the door. Before she could take another step, the Beastie lunged forward, and its claws ripped through cloth and skin, causing an agonized shriek to escape her throat as hot blood poured down her side.

Mary screamed and screamed…

CHAPTER 2
QUEEN, PRINCESS & KNIGHT

BANG!!

"Darn, these rats!" Mam threw her rolling pin at a huge rat as it squeezed through a hole in the wall, its long, scaly tail trailing behind it.

"Honest to *God*, if I was a cat, I'd chew off its big, fat b…"

"Please don't swear like that, Mam," said Mary, from across the tidy kitchen with its pretty blue curtains. She dusted the flour off her hands upon her red apron, frowning at the lump of dough in front of her, dark hair swept back behind her ears.

"Are you alright, girl?" Mam glanced her way, noting her daughter's tone. "Bad night again?"

"Nothing to worry about, Mam," said Mary, forcing a smile. "Just another dream." She rubbed her side absently and looked at Tom in his baby chair, squishing a piece of bread in his chubby hands. Her nightmares were happening a lot lately and getting more vivid every night.

"Can't even remember what it was about. Probably being scratched by a big ugly rat!"

"You'd tell me if something's the matter, right?"

"'Course, Mam."

No matter how clean they kept their little apartment, rats were a constant headache. That was because the rest of the flat was wet and dingy, perfect for breeding dirty rats, cockroaches, and other disgusting creatures.

Not only that, Mary and her mother had to climb seventy-seven steps, stepping on moldy carpets to reach the top floor where their apartment was, as they had no elevator.

As for the other tenants in the building, there were a few decent folks they were friendly with, but unfortunately, they also had more than their fair share of crooks, scoundrels, and other unsavory characters as neighbors.

"Stay away from the window, dear," Mam would say. "I don't want any of those rascals looking at you." Even with the freezing weather and heavy snow, there were always people loitering in the streets, mostly hooded men, talking in hushed voices and smoking foul-smelling cigarettes. They had dirty faces and even dirtier looks whenever they glanced up at their window.

Mam could not stand those types of people, but she hated the rats even more. She could not bear their beady eyes, twitchy noses, and horrid flea-bitten bodies. No matter how many traps they laid, the mischievous critters were too clever and were always heard scampering beneath the floorboards and behind the walls.

One particularly nasty rat was caught chewing on poor Tom's right ear, leaving a jagged scar, so he had to sleep with Mam ever since. As an additional safety measure, Mam resorted to keeping her rolling pin under her pillow. Her *Mickey Masher,* she called the heavy piece of oak, twirling it about expertly with one hand, and many a time, Mary actually felt sorry for the rats that came within striking, or throwing, distance.

BANG! WHOMP! THUMP! A squished rat here, a bashed rat there; Mam could be very accurate with the *Mickey Masher.*

In truth, apart from her nightmares, the annoying rats and unsavory characters who kept Mam constantly worried, to little Mary, who always looked at the bright side of things through her gentle brown eyes, there was nowhere else she would rather be. Her home was her castle. She was the princess, Mam the stern but kind queen, and Tom with his big blue eyes and curly brown hair, the chivalrous knight who would one day wield his magic sword into battle against evil, or at least stop chewing on his big toe.

We mentioned earlier that people prayed hard during that dark, frosty period. Mary was one of those. Actually, to be more precise, she made wishes. Mary would make two in particular. The first wish was always for her family, and her second wish was to keep those stinky rats away.

***

"SSSSHHHHHHH!!!"

Mam stood as still as a rock, finger to lips, doughnut bun hairdo quivering like jelly, indicating she would tolerate nothing but absolute silence, ears strained near the slim wall separating their apartment from that of their immediate neighbors, the Waterstones.

"What do you think I am, a walking cash machine??!!" shouted a high-pitched male voice.

"No Ted, *No!!* You're definitely *not* a walking cash machine. You are a self-centered, selfish…" countered a shrill female voice before they heard a *CRASH* and a yell from Ted.

Every morning, for the past three years since the Waterstones moved in, Mam would religiously keep up with their marital discourse. In fact, such was Mam's obsession that if she missed even one episode, she would spend the entire day moping around in utter misery.

Apart from this particular compulsion of her Mam's, without ever thinking about it, Mary would copy her in everything else: the way she walked, the way she talked, even the way she carried Tom and sang him to sleep.

One of the favorite things Mam used to do before she hurt her back was baking. So, Mary loved baking, too. She would wear her red apron, just like Mam's, though quite a bit smaller. She would bake all kinds of goodies, like muffins, tarts, cookies, and cakes, depending on what ingredients were available during the days of rationing.

But bread was Mary's specialty. By her tenth birthday, Mam said Mary was so good she could work at the baker's shop whenever it opened its doors again. But Mary always replied she would rather just bake for Mam and Tom. Mam used to be a nurse but had suffered a nasty fall just after Tom was born, so she spent most of her time resting at home.

"Let me do the baking, Mam, you just sit with the baby," Mary would say after breakfast. She knew her mammy's back was particularly sore in the mornings. Mam would then give Mary her best smile and mind

Tom, who kept doing what small boys his age like to do: grabbing, chewing, and babbling at the top of their voices.

Every time Mary finished baking a loaf of bread, Mam would take the two crusty ends first (affectionately called *The Crusty Butts*, which always made Mary laugh) and leave the soft middle part for Mary and Tom. "The *Crusty Butts* are the best bits," Mam always said.

They would spread a bit of salted butter or marmalade on their slices or, more often than not, dunk them in a cup of tea or hot chocolate. Tom loved bread too, but he would crush them in his chubby hands before stuffing the mushed pieces into his mouth or flinging them away, making a frightful mess each time. Mary would help with the cleaning up, making sure she swept every bit of crumb so the rats would not get any.

***

"Mam," Mary said one morning. "We only have a bit of flour left in the bag."

"I'll get us some more soon, dearest," said Mam, her eyes strained but with a smile on her lips which gladdened Mary's heart.

"Don't you be worrying about it, Mam. I'll just make a baby-sized bread this time!"

So, Mary started to work, wearing her special red

apron, the sleeves of her shirt rolled above her elbows, and her long dark hair secured with a headband. Then, she poured the flour into a baking dish, to which she added a touch of salt, baking powder, and some water.

After an hour, the dough had risen, and with a little bit of help from Mam with the oven, Mary baked the most mouth-watering loaf of white bread, baby-sized, of course. It had the proportions of a small pillow, with a crusty outer skin and a soft, fluffy flesh. When Mary poked the bread with a knife, it went straight through like butter. The smell was so delicious, even Tom stopped chewing his toes and stared, drooling all over his top.

"Tadaaaa…!" Mary proudly announced she had just baked her masterpiece and that she could do no better. "I was in the zone," she explained to Mam and Tom with all seriousness.

"We'll leave this on the table to cool. We must make sure to leave a slice for Aunt Kay. You know how much she loves your bread."

"Amongst other things," said Mary, a naughty twinkle in her eye.

"Now, now, Mary. You know I don't like you saying anything bad about…" then they both burst out laughing.

They were actually very fond of Aunt Kay (a

glamorized version of Karen). Still, in her late thirties, she was a couple of years older than Mam. She lived alone in another flat a few blocks away.

Aunt Kay had a few unwholesome habits and tendencies, which Mam was very keen to protect her one and only daughter from: smoking and an objectionable fashion sense, amongst others. She would frequently spend more time in their small apartment rather than her own, taking over their couch.

But for all that, Aunt Kay was the one who was always there for them, ready to lend a helping hand, especially since Mam hurt her back.

"Nobody's perfect," Mam would say to Mary whenever her defensive sisterly instincts take over, "but she's the perfect aunt for you."

***

The Beastie looked up at the brightly lit window from his vigil on the dark pavement below. Hands in his coat pockets, he stood still, swaying gently in ecstasy. The tantalizing aroma of bread wafted down to his sharp nose, but it was another smell that his stirred his excitement, the metallic tang making him salivate, causing his stomach to grumble. The smell of a child's blood.

The snow fell steadily but appeared not to touch him, as if he was surrounded by a giant air bubble.

He was the hunter, and he delighted in stalking his prey. His chosen face twitched furiously with growing anticipation, the face he had learned from experience all children loved and trusted. The visage of a dear old man.

Tonight was the night. He was going to finally meet little Mary in the flesh. Ooo… how exciting! They would talk, laugh, and maybe play one of his favorite games, a game of wishes.

The Beastie inhaled deeply, savoring the sweet scent, and imagined plunging his canines into her delicate neck, gulping down the red juice, relishing every single drop…

"Spare change, please?"

A tall, skinny man shuffled drunkenly through the thick carpet of snow. He wore a filthy overcoat over his lanky frame, which reeked heavily of stale urine, corrupting the Beastie's heightened senses and spoiling his mood.

The man lumbered closer until he towered over the Beastie. He held out one withered hand as beggars do while the other gripped a wickedly sharp razor concealed under his long coat sleeve.

"Spare some change, please?" He gave a crazed laugh then, his gullet quivering visibly in his wrinkled neck, his crack-destroyed brain beyond reason.

The Beastie fixed his malevolent green eyes on the man.

"What are you, deaf?!! Give me money, I'm hungry!!" The man shrieked and raised his razor, ready to slash open the Beastie's face.

Quick as a snake, the Beastie leapt, growling in fury, and buried his sharp black teeth deep in the man's neck. In one fluid motion, he jerked his head back, ripping open the sinews and spraying blood in a wide arc across the white carpet.

The Beastie turned his head and spat out the mixture of flesh and vessels just as the man dropped to the snow, body convulsing violently.

I'm hungry too, but nothing spoils one's appetite more than old people's blood, he thought to himself. Without a backward glance, he wiped off the gore from his face with his sleeve and walked slowly towards Mary's flat, whistling a happy tune.

CHAPTER 3
THE ODDEST-LOOKING MAN

Face screwed up in fierce concentration, Mary used a bread knife to cut her loaf into five equal pieces: three *Fluffy Middles* and two *Crusty Butts*. She took four small plates from the cupboard and placed two *butts* on a plate for Mam and one *fluff* each for Tom, Aunt Kay, and herself.

"There, ready," said Mary. "When do you think Aunt Kay would be here, Mam?"

"Oh, I'm sure she'll be here whenever she's hungry."

Just then, there came the sound of someone knocking at the door.

Knock…

Knock…

Knock…

"There, that's probably her now."

Strange, thought Mary. *Why didn't she just use the spare key, like she always does?*

Mary went to the door and, because she was still small, stood on a stool to look through the peephole. She could see the carpeted landing but did not see anybody out there. She was about to say so when the knocking came again.

Knock…

Knock…

Knock…

"Open the door, dear," said Mam.

Mary peered through the peephole again, her hand grasping the door handle tightly, a familiar twitch of anxiety clutching her stomach.

"There's no one there, Mam," said Mary.

Mam went to the door and, without bothering to use the peephole, hauled it open. Just as Mary had said, there was no one outside.

"It's those pesky kids again. They ducked their heads so you couldn't see them. *Eejits!*" She slammed the door shut. Mam had a bit of a temper when it came to stuff like that.

Tom jumped in fright and started bawling at the top of his voice. Mam gave a huge sigh and went over to comfort him. She sat on the bed with him and started to sing softly.

Mary turned to sit on the couch when she noticed something very strange; a hush had suddenly fallen over them. Mary looked over to where Mam was sitting very still with Tom. Her long dark hair was covering them both, so she could not see their faces. Tom had stopped crying, and Mam was no longer singing. The clatter of the wind on the windowpanes had subsided, and there were none of the usual noises from the streets and neighbors.

Fear clutched Mary's throat. She felt nauseous as a dull ache spread down her side. She could feel her heart beating fast, making a loud galloping sound in her ears.

Thump-thump…

Thump-thump…

Thump…

"Mam?" Mary found it hard to breathe.

Mam sat still as a statue, face downcast.

Maybe Mam is afraid Tom would start crying again? Mary wondered.

Knock…

Knock…

Knock…

Mary tip-toed over to the door, stood on her stool, and peeped through. She still could not see anyone out there, but this time, Mary thought she saw a small shadow just at the edge of her vision.

Mam's right. It is those pesky kids again, thought Mary. *This is my home, and I won't be scared! I'm double digits now, so I'll give them such an earful for being an awful nuisance and disturbing our dinner!*

Mary, being her Mam's daughter, could have a bit of a temper, too.

Mary unlocked the door, stepped down from her stool, and opened the door.

There, standing just outside the doorway, was the oddest-looking man she had ever seen. He was no taller than her, with white bushy eyebrows, a long, hooked nose, and a greasy, grey beard that reached down to his tummy. He wore a crumpled, dark green three-piece suit and matching bowler hat. He did not smell very nice, like he had not washed for a long time. Mary was so astonished that she just stood staring at him.

"Didn't your mother ever tell you it's not polite to stare?" grumbled the strange little man.

"Oh. Pardon me," said Mary, taken off guard. "May I help you?"

"That's better!" He smiled very wide, showing rotten, stumpy teeth. He stepped closer, piercing her with his cold, green eyes. Mary had to resist wrinkling her nose at his horrid stench.

"I was just passing by when I came across the most mouth-watering fragrance of baked bread. My nose, which has never been wrong, mind you, led me here. You must be the very best baker in the whole wide world!"

Mary was very pleased. She had never been praised like that before. This queer man must be very nice, even if he could use a bath.

"I am so very hungry. I've been wondering the streets in this frightful weather all day, hoping to find a kind-hearted soul to spare me a bite to eat." He grinned again and stared at Mary hungrily.

Mary looked at his large black boots and thought it strange they appeared quite dry, and he did not seem to have any snow on his hat or coat. She dismissed the notion and took pity on this old man.

"Well, we've barely enough for ourselves, but you could have half of mine." She was not going to give this man Mam's piece even though she had two *butts*.

"Why, thank you. So kind, so very kind of you. May I please come in?"

"I'm sorry, but my Mam wouldn't like that. If you stay here, I'll be right back with your bread." Mary did not notice a flash of rage cross the man's face. She went inside to her plate and broke her piece of bread into two. She handed one to the old man.

Surprisingly, he did not eat it straight away but placed it in his coat's inner pocket.

"Now, for showing me such incredible generosity, it is my turn to do you a favor." He reached out and, with a long, dirty fingernail, traced a line down Mary's cheek. She stood frozen as the dull ache in her side began to throb painfully.

"Please don't…"

"But why? As you'd probably guessed, I am no ordinary man. In fact, I am very, very special! Indeed, I am one in a million, a billion… gazillion! You might say I'm like Santa with my long white beard!" He ran his filthy fingers through his greasy beard.

"Children love Santa, you know, Ho… Ho… Ho! But I'm better, much better than Santa. You see, I have magic, just like the genie from Aladdin's lamp! So, kind, pretty girl, I will grant you three wishes! Just tell me anything you want, and I will grant it!"

Mary's vision blurred as a thick, sickly smell wafted up her nostrils. *Where have I seen this man before?*

"Maybe you'd like a new dress, a new pair of shoes, or a nice ribbon to tie your hair with? I say, I can't help noticing this shirt you're wearing. Is blue your favorite color, little Mary?"

Mary's head swum as she nodded. *How did he know*

my name?

For the first time, she noticed the man had pointy ears beneath his bowler hat, ears that belonged to magical pixies and other fairy folk that she had read about in her books. But Mary did not believe a word he was saying. He seemed quite mad to her, more like the Mad Hatter than Santa.

It wouldn't hurt to try, thought Mary. She would give him something easy to do, then maybe he would go away. She did not like this man; there was something not right with his eyes, the way he was looking at her.

"Ok, then. I wish for a bag of the nicest flour."

"Hah! Is that it, flour? For baking? So easy! So very easy! As you wish! One down, two to go! And be sure to let me in the door next time, won't you, little Mary?" He gave her one last leering grin, then snapped his fingers.

SNAP!!!

At once, there came the sound of Tom crying loudly. Mary turned to find her Mam cradling Tom and soothing his hair back. She looked back to see if the man had her flour, but he had already vanished, leaving behind an unpleasant smell of rot.

As soon as she closed the door, Mary felt a peculiar pressure at the back of her head. Still holding the handle, she saw a vision of a large predatory animal, grunting and barking madly as it jumped high over a black wall, disappearing from view. Her last thoughts were *Mam, there's something I need to tell you…*

"Mary? You ok, girl?"

The pressure in her head disappeared suddenly, and with it, a chunk of Mary's memories crumbled away.

By the time she walked back to her Mam, Mary had no recollection of the odd-looking man. So, it came as a complete surprise to her that when they finally sat down to sample the bread, she found half her piece was missing.

"I hope it wasn't those darn rats again," said Mam, eying her *Mickey Masher*. "Never mind, dear. You could have one of my *Crusty Butts* if you like."

***

CRASH!!

The door burst open as a whirlwind of fizzy blonde hair, bright make-up, and fake fur strode through the door, wearing a pair of high-heeled leather boots. "I swear, those stairs would be the death of me!!"

"Morning Kay," said Mam.

"Aunt Kay! We missed you last night," said Mary.

"Of course, you missed me! So, how's my *favorite* niece this morning?"

"I'm your *only* niece," Mary giggled.

"And how's my *only* favorite nephew?" Aunt Kay looked for Tom, who was being potty trained and straining on his potty chair.

"Never mind, Tommy boy, I see you're quite busy at the moment. So, any news?"

"You missed Mary's masterpiece yesterday," said Mam. "It was her *bestest* bread ever. Where were you, by the way?"

"*Mmmm,* out and about," said Aunt Kay with a long-lashed wink at Mary before checking her lipstick in her hand-held mirror. She caught Mam staring at her. "What?!"

"Nothing. It's just that… you have to be the only person with a tan in the middle of the worst snowstorm *ever* in Dublin."

"Watch your mouth, Ger! I'm certainly *not* the only one." Mary giggled again.

"So how are you, little Mary?" said Aunt Kay, running her long fingernails through Mary's hair.

"Good. We ate your share last night. I'd bake another one, but we're out of flour."

"I'll get some more, dear," said Mam quickly.

"Not to worry. *Super Kay* to the rescue…!" She produced, with a flourish, a bag of whole wheat flour from her carrier bag.

"That's so crazy, Aunt Kay! How did you know?"

"To be honest, I *didn't* know. I was looking for my coffee this morning, and I found this just lying there in the cupboard. Hope it's not expired or anything. *Please* just take it. Nails and baking don't go too well together, you know."

"*Yay!*" Mary grabbed the flour and started getting the cutlery ready.

"You need to get out more, my dear," said Aunt Kay.

"*Kayy...*" warned her sister.

"Isn't she supposed to start dating by now? How old is she again, twelve?"

"She just turned ten, as you very well know! We had her party last week!"

"You're missing the point, though. I had my first date when I was just about her age. Or was it seven? Can't really remember."

Mam did not bother replying.

"I'll take her out for a walk later if you like. You know, the snow and hail would do her a *world* of good. It can't be healthy for a child to be spending so much time with her mother like this."

"You're afraid we might actually bond together?"

"You're darn right! I never bonded with our

mammy, and look how I turned out?"

They heard the wind knocking against the windowpanes for several seconds.

"Ger, have you heard the news?"

"Which one?"

"What do you mean, which one?! Everyone's scared to death with all these kidnappings! Kids going missing everywhere!"

"I know that. It's scary, but I thought..."

"Darn right, it's scary! You better watch these two like a hawk. But it isn't just kids. Pets, you know, like dogs, cats, have gone missing, too."

"Surely the Guards have found something already?"

"Not a thing! But I'm hearing such horrible things; seems it's worse here in town. Just up the road, someone's lost their child not a week ago. Surely, you must've heard. No? Well, apparently, the parents woke up one morning, and he was just gone, vanished into thin air! I think that's the third one this month. It's brutal! I'm not one for having kids, but it breaks my heart to hear these things."

Aunt Kay sat down heavily on the sofa.

"Are you ok there, honey?" Mam said to Mary, who was busy measuring out the flour into a dish on the kitchen table. "All good, Mam," said Mary with a thumbs up, face screwed in concentration.

"C'mere, you're not listening to me, Ger. Where was I?"

"Your heart's broken?"

"What? Anyway, here's the really scary bit. *Oooh!* I get goosebumps just thinking about it... maybe I shouldn't tell you..."

Mam got up to help Mary.

"Ok, I'll tell you. They say that just before a child goes missing, they hear the sound of someone, or *something*, knocking on the doors and windows, like wanting to come in."

"That's really creepy."

"Yeah, who knocks on doors anymore? Haven't they heard of doorbells?"

"But *who's* been knocking on people's doors?"

"That's just it! Nobody has seen anything yet, except..."

"Except what?"

"Oh, I'm too scared to go on... Ok, ok. Apparently, there's been sightings of a creepy old man with a long beard and pointy ears peeping through windows, but he'd be gone before you got a proper look at him."

"What! Like some sort of *Leprechaun*? That's just

mad! It's probably some nutter or something."

"Who knows what's what these days. But you're right, there's really sick people out there who won't think twice about hurting kids… just be careful, ok?"

Mam smiled. "Ok, don't worry, Mary's a good girl; she tells me *everything*."

Do you, now, little Mary? A harsh whisper close to Mary's ear.

Mary's eyes suddenly went wide open, and her hand started to shake as she held a wooden spoon. She looked up from the worktable to the back of her Mam's head. She watched in horror as long, dirty fingernails emerged forth, parting her Mam's dark hair. A pair of green malevolent eyes was staring right at her.

Mary tried to shout a warning but only managed a croak; her throat felt constricted, as if a powerful hand had reached out and squeezed her windpipe. *There's' something I need to tell you, Mam. I'm trying to be the good daughter like you want me to be, but my brain's all fuzzy. There's someone trying to hurt me…*

Dark furry hands ripped apart her Mam's head, and the grotesque face of the Beastie leered at her, green tongue wagging hungrily. Mary dropped the spoon with a clatter.

"You ok, honey?" said Aunt Kay, her eyes glued to

an article in a magazine.

At once, Mary sucked in air deeply. She shook her head and blinked rapidly, surprised she had dropped her spoon. Her Mam turned back and smiled at her.

"I'm fine, just clumsy, that's all." Mary picked up her spoon and went back to her baking. The nightmare was wiped from her memory. She started humming a merry tune.

Aunt Kay leaned back on her chair and sighed. "A small man with a big pot of gold couldn't be that bad, though, right?"

"Speaking of a small man with a pot of gold..." Mam sighed and went to clean up Tom.

CHAPTER 4
CROOKS & SCOUNDRELS

"Don't grow up too quickly, baby!"

Mary stared at Tom, who was standing on his chubby legs, holding on to Mam's skirt, a cheeky smile lighting his round face.

"Soon, he'll be running around the place and making a bigger mess," Mam said as she ironed their clothes. Mary recalled fondly how Tom had looked when he was just born, lying in his cot like a tiny, shriveled teddy bear.

"You know, Mam. I'm not sure whether what you said about me eating bread crusts would really make my straight hair go curly. I mean, it's been nearly a year and… Mam?"

Mary turned to check on her Mam, who was sitting on the sofa and staring into space, Tom lying unmoving by her side, his blue eyes wide open. Silence suddenly enveloped their apartment. The sound of the wind vanished, and so did the usual hustle and bustle from the streets below.

Knock…

Knock…

Knock…

Sudden dread spread through Mary at the sound. Her heart thudded painfully against her thin chest as a wave of dizziness caused her to lurch on her feet.

Weak moonlight streamed through the window, and shadows darkened every corner as Mary stood shakily on a stool and looked through the peephole. The top of a bowler hat was bopping up and down in her lower field of vision.

What was it that Aunt Kay said the other day? Oh, how I wish my brain isn't so mushy. Something about missing children and a stranger that goes around knocking on doors. But what should I do? Anyway, it might be someone looking for help, and Mam is always saying we should help people."

As Mary slowly turned the door handle, a slip of memory trickled back in fits and starts. She remembered giving bread to a nice, old man who, in turn, had helped her family get more flour.

Mary opened the door. "You shouldn't be back here. I'm not allowed to talk to strangers."

"But surely, I'm no longer a stranger? I know your name, don't I? I know your favorite color. Only friends know that. I'm a good friend, too; I make your wishes come true! Why, Mary, I even brought you flour so you could make more of your yummy bread, remember?"

Mary nodded her head in a daze.

"May I come in this time?" said the man, grinning from ear to ear, greedy eyes boring into Mary's as a trickle of saliva dripped from his bearded lips.

Something flashed in Mary's mind, a warning, and she stumbled back a step. She gagged as a sharp whiff of his stench pierced her nostrils, and her memory of him did not seem so nice anymore. He looked different, too, more menacing with his eyes closer set like a predatory animal's, his flat nose flaring with each rapid breath.

"You're not allowed in! If you're hungry, stay here while I fetch you something."

Mary did not notice the black thunder that flickered across the man's face as she returned to the kitchen and cut him a piece of bread. As she handed it to him, the man grabbed her hand in his hairy paw. Mary quivered at his clammy touch.

He smiled again, showing stumpy rotten teeth, before letting go and placing the bread in his inner coat pocket.

"So very kind! Thank you very much. What a good little girl you are! Like I promised, I am here to grant you your second wish. Ask me anything, my sweet Mary."

Mary did not want to make another wish. She did not want to talk to this weird little man anymore and wanted him to go away. Mary wanted to ask Mam what to do, but her mother was not paying attention.

Maybe Mam is worried about those crooks and scoundrels again, smoking as they look up at our window? Mary's confused brain was telling her.

Then suddenly, Mary had a bright idea: they did not have to put up with the hooligans anymore; she could simply wish them all away!

Why oh why didn't I think about this before? Mary thought, so annoyed with herself.

"For my second wish, make all the bad folks around the flat go away, far away from here," Mary said to the man.

He rubbed his glands gleefully. "Your wish is my command! But next time, I will have what I want, little Mary. And you will give it to me. Two wishes down, one to go!"

He snapped his filthy fingers loudly.
SNAP!!!

"Mary," called Mam. "Would you close the door,

please? There's such an awful draught." Mam's voice seemed to come from a great distance, and she felt a dull, throbbing sensation at the back of her head.

Mary stood holding onto the door handle, staring at the empty landing.

What am I doing here?

"Sure, Mam."

Mary closed the door.

"Are you alright, dear? You look like you've just seen a ghost!" Tom suddenly cried in a high-pitched voice from where he was lying. Mam picked him up and started crooning softly.

"I'm fine, Mam," Mary whispered.

***

The clock struck midnight.

Mary opened her eyes and stared at the ceiling. It had taken Mam a long time to settle Tom earlier.

Strange, Tom was such a good baby; he had never cried like that before.

It had scared Mary to see her brother like that, worse to see her Mam so worried. Never mind… at least Tom did stop crying and was now sleeping soundly next to Mam.

Tap…

Tap…

Tap…

Oh no… That awful sound again. Am I dreaming?

Mary tried to sit up but lay frozen in her single bed, able to only blink her eyes. Her throat felt like dry parchment; her breaths caught in her chest as she tried desperately to move.

Stay calm, stay calm. This is just another nightmare. You'll wake up soon.

Mary found she could move her eyes. She looked to her right at her cupboard mirror. It was not so dark that she could make out its outline and shiny silhouette.

Tap…

Tap…

Tap…

Was it her imagination, or was that the shadow of someone knocking on the other side of her mirror? The shadow of a short man wearing a hat.

"You can't come in," mumbled Mary weakly.

A guttural scream reverberated from the mirror as it shattered into a million pieces.

"Do you want to know what happened to all those missing children, little Mary?"

The Beastie stepped through the portal, goat-hide boots crunching the broken glass.

"Before you answer that, I was just mulling over

another question: am I an 'it' or a 'he'? Hmmm… Am I more beast than man? I much prefer 'he' though; sounds more civilized, don't you think?"

The Beastie was waving something at her as he stepped closer until his grotesque half-man, half-pig visage came into her field of vision. She could see his dirty, grey beard was blotched by a dark liquid. His face hovered over hers, and the drops dribbled down onto her face.

Waves of revulsion forced hot vomit up her throat as the sharp metallic tang of blood filled her nostrils. Something wet slapped against her neck and chest. Only when the Beastie dangled it in front of her did she realize it was a severed child's arm, the blood still warm against her skin.

"Two wishes down, little Mary!"

Mary screamed in terror as darkness enveloped her.

CHAPTER 5
PEEKABOO

"What are you doing there, Mam?" asked Mary.

Mam was standing with her left ear pressed tight against the kitchen wall, anxiously biting her lower lip.

"*Shhh!!* Quiet."

Mary tip-toed over and mimicked her Mam, pressing her left ear a few feet below. After a couple of minutes, Mary whispered, "What are we doing again, Mam?"

Mam gave a groan. "I'm just dying to know what Vilma's going to do."

She stepped away from the wall and smiled guiltily at Mary. "It's not polite to eavesdrop, girl. Remember Mam's golden rule: DO WHAT I SAY, NOT WHAT I DO, ok?"

"I thought the golden rule was, "MAMMY KNOWS BEST, SO SHUT YOUR TRAP OR I'LL GIVE

YOU A SMACK BOTTOM."

"That's the second golden rule."

Mam sighed, "But it's been *three* days now and not a peep from Ted and Vilma. The tension is driving me crazy!"

Tom was in his roller, happily munching on a finger biscuit and babbling loudly. Mary rubbed his head and went to look out the window.

"Stay away from the window, honey. Haven't we discussed this already?"

"But there's no one out there, Mam. Come look."

They both gazed out at the mid-morning landscape from the window. A grey overcast provided a stark contrast to the white pristine snow blanketing the rooftops, street, and pavement as if an artist had only black and white on her pastel to paint a portrait of the city.

A palpable silence enveloped the scene, the screeching of birds and howling of the wind the only sounds to be heard.

"Strange. Where is everybody?"

At this time, there would usually be some folk already out and about. There was nobody in the street outside their window, not even any footprints.

Mam opened the window and craned her neck to

look at the other nearby apartments and streets beyond theirs. To her relief, she could see there the usual hustle and bustle of life. It was just their immediate vicinity that seemed deserted.

Mam was just about to close the window when something caught her eye. Across the street to her right, a creature was lurking behind a corner of the opposite building, looking up at them. It stood on four powerful legs and, from that distance, had the appearance of a large hairy pig but with the longer jaws of a canine.

Mary saw it, too, and knew the creature was staring right at her. She shuddered with fear. Her head swam, and her stomach constricted painfully.

"I've never seen a dog that size," muttered Mam.

The creature took a few steps forward and dropped what looked like a large piece of bone in its jaws onto the soft snow, which immediately turned red.

Mary shuddered violently as she realized this was the same monster from her nightmares.

"That's a large bone it's chewing."

That's no bone, Mam, the words not bypassing Mary's throat.

Tom started wailing, his voice unusually high-pitched, as if he was hurt or very frightened about something.

"Step back from the window, Mary!" cried Mam as she hurried to pick Tom up. Mary stood petrified, her gaze locked with the Beastie's.

I got rid of all the baddies for you, little Mary, just as you wished. One more to go…

Mary heard the hoarse, feral voice in her head as the Beastie spoke directly to her. She could see he was grinning, his fangs and long green tongue visible in his bloody maw.

Didn't take much persuasion, those crooks and scoundrels. A bite here, a snip there, and they all just hot-footed away! Well, speaking of a hot foot…

The Beastie chuckled as he began tearing away at the remains of a human leg, the guttural sounds clear in the still morning air.

Mam pulled Mary away, and she gulped in air deeply. She did not realize she was holding her breath for so long.

Mam closed the curtains. Mary reeled back and sat heavily on a stool. She envisioned a dark wall in the center of her brain and the Beastie jumping over it, lost from view. Just as before, bits of her memory dissipated, and she had no recollection of the monster.

"Somebody should lock that mad dog away before somebody gets hurt," said Mam.

"Hmmm?" Mary mumbled absently.

A sudden thought struck Mam. "Mary, wait here and mind Tom for me; I'll only be a sec."

"Where are you going?"

"I just want to check out something," said Mam, putting on her jumper and shoes.

"Don't leave us here, Mam."

"Don't be silly. I'll be back in a jiffy."

"No, Mam, I'm scared," pleaded Mary.

Mam looked at Mary in surprise. She had never seen Mary look so upset before. "Ok, just put on your jumper. We won't be going outside."

When Mary was ready, Mam carried Tom and, at an impulse, decided to bring the *Mickey Masher*. They came out onto the landing and listened. There were two other apartments sharing the third floor. To Mam's surprise, both doors were slightly ajar. She went to the nearest one.

"Hallo… anybody home? Ted? Vilma?" She rang the doorbell and rapped on the door. The door swung inwards. The three remained outside and waited. They could see the cluttered living room and part of the kitchen, with cutlery left unwashed in the sink.

There did not seem to be anything too out of the ordinary. Mam felt goosebumps all over her body, with a mixture of nervousness and curiosity. She took a step inside the door and jumped in shock when she felt Mary's hand on her arm. Mary gave a quick shake of her head, indicating she did not want to go in any further.

They backed out, leaving the door open, and approached the other apartment. Mam did not ring the bell or knock this time, somehow feeling the need to avoid making any noise. She pushed the door inwards, which creaked on its hinges. The apartment belonged to a French couple, who sometimes shared honeyed crepes with them.

"*Bonjour!*... It's just us... hello..." said Mam, anxiety keeping her voice low.

"Let's go back," said Mary, tugging on her jumper.

"Just a second, honey. I need to make sure they're ok."

Mam took a deep breath and walked straight in. With Tom held in one arm, the *Masher* held in the other hand, and Mary close behind, she quickly scanned the kitchen and living room. Her eyes rested briefly on a framed photo of the young couple beaming in front of the Eiffel Tower. The double bed looked recently slept in.

They went back out into the corridor, Mam's forehead creased in worry. She descended partway down the steps to where she could have a view of the apartments on the floor below. She peered at the partially opened doors, straining to hear anything. In all her years living in that flat, she had never known the place to be this quiet before. Even Tom had had to get used to sleeping through all the usual shouting, banging, and music blaring.

"We need to check on Mrs. Brennan, honey," Mam said to Mary.

Mrs. Brennan was an old widow who lived on the ground floor. Her husband died when Mary was just a couple of years old. She always seemed gruff, but Mary overheard Mam saying it was because she hardly saw her own children since they had moved out.

So, the three went further down, bypassing the second floor. Mrs. Brennan's door was closest to the front door. This one was closed. Mam tried the handle and found it unlocked. The room inside was gloomy; the thick curtains drawn closed.

"Mrs. Brennan? Are you in there?" called Mam from the doorway. "It's me, Ger, from upstairs, with little Mary and Tom."

Mam stepped inside and flicked on the light switch. A sour smell filled the room. She recalled the last time they were in here, a few weeks ago, to drop off a blanket. The place was bright and airy then, with the pleasant aroma of rose talcum powder.

They explored the kitchen and living room. "Mam, look," said Mary, pointing to a walking stick lying half concealed under the couch. A cold sweat broke out on Mam's forehead. The old lady would never go out of the apartment without the walking stick to support her arthritic hip.

With mounting dread, she led Mary to the bedroom. The room had no window. Mam turned on the switch here, but the light was not working. Mary let out a whimper as their eyes adjusted to the gloom. The shape of a prone figure lay on the single bed under the blanket. Mam could not help noticing the checkered pattern of the fleece blanket which they had gifted Mrs. Brennan.

They approached the bed slowly, fear slowing every step. The sour stench became stronger the closer they got. Mam reached out a trembling hand and clutched the top edge of the blanket. Taking a deep breath, she yanked the blanket off…

"Peekabooo…!"

"AaaaaaaAAAAAGGGGGHHHHHHhhhhh!!!!!"
Mam flung away the *Mickey Masher* while, thankfully, keeping a hold on Tom, who started bawling. Mary simply whimpered fearfully.

"Kay! I swear to God! I'll…"

Aunt Kay was standing at the bedroom door. "What the heck are you guys doing here? I went upstairs, and you were gone. I was just on my way out when I saw you from the corridor going into this room."

Mam sat down shakily on the bed, hugging Tom, Mary looking very pale even in the gloom. Under the blanket was a thick wool jacket they sometimes see Mrs. Brennan wearing. It looked like the lady also wore it in bed. The jacket was damp and was the source of the sour smell.

"Where is everybody?" said Aunt Kay. "This whole place is dead."

"We'll talk later. Here, you carry Tom. "I need a strong cup of tea."

***

Aunt Kay made a hot, steaming pot, adding extra tea bags and big spoonfuls of sugar. "Don't drink any of this stuff, girl," she said to Mary. "You'd get high as a kite."

Mary was sipping her own cup of hot cocoa, Tom fast asleep in his cot.

"I can't make heads or tails of this," said Mam. "Was there an evacuation last night, a gas leak or something? Maybe we slept through an earthquake, and everyone just left without us."

"Looks like you got what you've always wanted.

You have the building to yourselves now," said Aunt Kay.

Mary looked down into her mug and did not reply.

"Kay, did you see a big, ugly-looking dog outside?"

"What dog?"

Mary's eyes suddenly rolled up in her head, and she dropped her mug. She gasped and banged her fist on the side of her head.

Mam looked at her in alarm. "Mary! What is it? Stop that!"

Mary squeezed her eyes tight and clutched her head. "My brain hurts!" She hammered her head again.

"A headache? I'll get you a painkiller," said Aunt Kay.

"No!" moaned Mary.

"What is it, dear? Tell mammy!"

Mary curled up on the couch, arms covering her face.

Mam stood to comfort her, but Kay pulled her back. "Leave her be, Ger," she whispered. "I think she's having a migraine attack."

"What!? Mary doesn't have migraine."

"Here, put this on her," said Aunt Kay, grabbing a blanket from the bedroom.

They watched anxiously over Mary, who was still

lying curled up, covering her face. Soon, her breathing eased as she snored softly.

"We should take her to the doctor," said Aunt Kay. Mam nodded.

They sat in silence. The weather changed abruptly, the light dimming and thunder rumbling in the distance. Soon after came the sharp clicks of hail stones pummelling the window.

Mary groaned softly in her sleep, then, eyes still closed, she pushed her right palm out as if warding off something. "No! Stop!" she cried. "Stop now!"

Mam came to her side and placed her hand on Mary's forehead. Mary opened her eyes and stared blankly for a few seconds before recognizing her mother.

"You were having a nightmare, honey. Do you feel sick?"

Mary shook her head. "I'm ok. I was very scared when we went downstairs. I feel better now."

"What were you dreaming about?" asked Aunt Kay.

Mary shook her head. "I don't remember."

"It's ok," said Mam, giving her forehead a kiss. "Bad dreams are best forgotten anyway. I'll make you more hot cocoa."

Mam felt Mary's forehead again. "You don't feel

hot, so that's good."

Mary rested her head back on the couch and watched Mam as she made the hot cocoa. What she could not tell them was that she kept seeing a dark wall, and there was something hiding behind it, something bad, really, really bad.

Chapter 6
The Giant Spear

"There she is, Luv, the pride of Dublin! What do you think, beautiful, isn't she?"

Aunt Kay and Mary were out for a walk while Mam took a nap with Tom. They were facing the mighty Monument of Light. Four hundred feet of impeccable architectural feat, layers upon layers of solid steel in the shape of a giant spear, an unshakable symbol of hope against the troubled times everyone was facing.

"Aunt Kay, it's just the Spire. I see it every day from our window."

"But *still*, we'd be lost without it. Literally, I couldn't find my way in all this snow if I didn't have that oversized pin to look out for."

Mary giggled.

"What's so funny?"

"Imagine if a giant fell back and sat on the Spire,

he'll have a…!"

"… a giant pain in the bum! Hah! Don't tell your mam I said that. It's your fault, by the way."

The streets were deserted. They were standing in front of the GPO, huddled together in their thick coats against the cold. The very few people they saw were all hurrying along, hands stuck in deeply in pockets, hoods all but concealing their faces.

Aunt Kay lit a cigarette and puffed out a cloud of smoke into the freezing air. She saw Mary gazing up at her. "I'm like a dragon, Mary. I need a bit of fire to keep my body warm," she said guiltily. Mary just kept staring as she puffed on her cigarette.

"This is my last pack, Mary, I swear. I'm always saying smoking is bad for you. It causes *premature facial wrinkles.*" Mary simply nodded.

"So, how's life treating you, my dear? Everything ok at home?"

Mary nodded again.

"I don't know how much you heard, what your Mam and I talked about the other day?"

"You mean about the missing children?"

"Yeah."

"And the weird, old man who knocks on people's doors?"

Aunt Kay shivered, and not just from the cold. She knelt down and looked into her niece's eyes to make sure she understood her next words.

"Be very, very careful, honey. There's lots of evil people around, even though they may not look so bad. Only trust your Mam and me. Don't ever talk to strangers, ok? And never, ever open the door to anyone without your Mam being there, understand?"

Mary nodded.

"Remember, I have the spare key to your apartment, so I would never need to knock or buzz. I just come in and annoy the hell out of your Mam."

Something touched Mary's memory then, a harsh whisper, a horrid scent, but it was gone before she could grab hold of it.

"Aunt Kay… I've been having these… nightmares."

Aunt Kay kept looking at her niece. "Go on."

"I can't remember them, but I'm scared to go sleep at night, on my own, but I'm double digits now, you know?"

Aunt Kay smiled at that.

"I used to have nightmares, too, dear. When I was about your age, I overheard my mam and her friend talk about this horrid monster that crept into people's houses and stole their food. I still remember what they said, that it had the face of a hog and the body of a small man. My mam didn't know I was listening to them. The worst thing was, my room was right next to our kitchen, and I would get really scared when it got dark."

Aunt Kay stood and brushed off the snow from her coat. "Your Mam knew, so she used to let me sleep with her."

"Do you still have the nightmares, Aunt Kay?"

Aunt Kay smiled. "Do you think I'd stay on my own if I do? I'm still scared of the dark, though. Let's keep walking. My butt's freezing!"

"At least it's not sore like the giant's!"

They walked quickly down Henry Street, keen to prolong their walk before heading back, passing shops that had been closed for months. The long rows of snow-covered buildings appeared as a long white valley, the howling gale forcing them to shout to be heard.

Aunt Kay looked down at her only niece. "As I grew older, the nightmares just fizzled out. I think, being a child, I was just very sensitive to everything. Even old wives' tales affected me quite badly. I'm sure your bad dreams would start to fizzle out, too, dear."

Mary smiled up at her aunt.

"You know what I miss most when I walk down here?" said Aunt Kay, throwing her cigarette butt into the snow.

"The juicy kebabs?" asked Mary.

"No. Those street buskers! I really miss their singing and loud music. Do you know any songs, Luv?"

Mary shook her head shyly.

"'Course you do. Everyone knows at least one song. You know what's your Mam's favorite? *Hey Jude* by The Beatles. She used to sing it all the time when we were kids. Drove me crazy!"

"I know that song," said Mary.

"Well, c'mon then, let's hear it!" said Aunt Kay.

Thus, together, hand in hand, they sang the song all the way down deserted Henry Street, with only the seagulls and pigeons as audiences, watching them pass with their starry eyes.

***

Now, *hold on.*

There was one other pair of eyes watching Aunt Kay and Mary as they trudged through the snow. Eyes still very sharp, though extremely ancient, glaring from a face that had changed many times over the millennia to suit its vile purpose.

The face belonged to a being that had thrived throughout mankind's gloomiest periods and prospered even during intervals of extreme human suffering: ice ages, wars and famine. For it, *he* was very clever, having observed humanity over generations, studying their weaknesses and desires. He knew whom to leave alone and whom to prey upon.

He had no true name but had been labeled many: *Goblin, Troll, Beastie*… different words describing the same creature. Beastie was his personal favorite, as the name more accurately described his dark nature, hibernating for decades in mountains and forests, awaiting the next great freeze before slithering out from his den.

The Beastie studied the pair as they passed from a window of a derelict building close to the Spire. His keen eyes were ever watchful, his ravenous nose constantly *sniff, sniff, sniffing*. For that was the way the Beastie hunted.

Once they had turned a corner, he shut the window and surveyed his quarters. The room comprised of a long, dark hall with a high ceiling. Fearful young eyes peeked out from behind rusty iron bars of cages lining one side as the Beastie leered at the children trapped within.

This building had been his most recent hideaway ever since he awoke from his long slumber at the start of the snowstorm, his existence going unnoticed by ordinary folk.

The Beastie had been weakened by prolonged

hunger and thirst as he initially crawled into his new lair, feeding upon rats and other small vermin. Eventually, as his powers grew, so did his appetite. From here, he roamed the city and outlying areas, journeying to more distant parts of the Emerald Isle in search of more substantial prey.

But he invariably returned to this sanctuary. He was the hunter, after all, and he missed the comforts of home, strewn as it was with the keepsakes from his countless prey.

The Beastie reached out and tapped the bar of the nearest cage with a long, dirty claw, causing the boy within to whimper with fear.

Tap…

Tap…

Tap…

The Beastie liked that tapping sound; for some reason, it gave him comfort beyond measure.

Moreover, whatever people may say regarding this monster, no one could fault his impeccable manners. He had long ago adopted the niceties of the human language, such as saying *please* and *thank you*. And he always, *always* knocked for permission before entering anyone's home.

Yes, of course, he spied on his chosen victims, but

that was out of necessity. It would not do for the grown-ups to gather in their numbers and chase him away. Would not do at all. And yes, the Beastie must admit, he relished toying with his victims' dreams, delighted in sensing their fear and terror even before they saw the Beastie in the flesh.

But above all else, he prided himself on his manners.

Anyway, those silly children had always opened their doors to let him in whenever he promised to make their wishes come true.

Until now. For the first time in his millennia-long experience, the Beastie encountered some resistance; he had never needed to grant more than one wish before the child's will broke, and he was able to enter.

Yet this Mary, an ordinary child like all the others for sure, but somehow she had been able to elude him so far.

But not to worry. They always let me in, little Mary, just as you will. Then I will feast upon your sweet marrow and your juicy baby brother's, too! Just one more wish to go…

The Beastie dipped his finger into a pile of white bone dust next to a grinding machine and started licking it with gusto, his green wet tongue quivering, all the while humming *Hey Jude,* which he also knew quite well.

CHAPTER 7
RUMPLESTILSKIN

Days went by, and gradually, Mary, Mam, and Tom became used to living on their own in that building, though they still kept their voices down at a respectable volume at night and would trudge carefully when going up and down the stairs out of habit.

Aunt Kay went to inform the Guards of the mysterious disappearance of all the people, and a series of investigations were conducted at the building.

"It sure is strange," said the officer, a tired but friendly looking man with a florid face and strikingly white teeth. "Unfortunately, the Missing Persons files are getting higher by the minute, and I don't really know when we would have time to sort this one out."

"Have there been any more missing children?" asked Mam.

"Nothing in the last few weeks, thank goodness,"

said the officer. "It's really distressing for everyone. I've got kids of my own, and I cannot even begin to imagine what the poor parents are going through." He thanked them after advising them to keep their doors and windows securely locked at all times.

***

Later that evening, Mam was reading a story to both Mary and Tom, who seemed to be listening attentively, lying on the bed, hands grabbing his feet.

The story was about a gentle maiden and her father, who had the foolish habit of spinning stories. For some obscure reason, the father decided to boast to anyone who would hear that his wonderful daughter could spin straw into gold. Of course, such a tale would spread far and wide, breeding envy among women and causing greed to flourish in men's hearts.

The news came to the ears of the king, who ordered the man and his daughter to be brought to his castle. He had already given instructions for a spinning wheel to be placed in three rooms, each room successively bigger than the other, all packed to the rafters with straw.

The king commanded the poor maiden to spin the straw into gold in the first room. He did not listen to her plea that her father was absolutely mad for ever suggesting such a thing, and he, as a monarch, was even more bonkers to believe her father.

Nevertheless, the king commanded the impossible deed to be done by sunrise the next morning. Otherwise, she and her braggart of a father would be executed. But, if the maiden was able to somehow pull off such a feat, the king would be gracious enough to make her his queen.

"Sounds like an awful father and a wicked king," interrupted Mary. "Who wants to be married to someone who'll hurt you if you don't do what he says?"

"They're supposed to be the good guys in this story, dear. The bad man is going to come up soon." So, Mam continued reading.

The miserable maiden sat weeping in the room next to the huge pile of straw, her father nowhere in sight.

"My dear father," she lamented. "Of all things to make up about me, you had to pick this one. Why didn't you say something sensible, like I could milk a cow with one hand in under a minute or spin cream to butter that *looks* like gold?"

The maiden's sorrowful cries were heard by a strange little man with a long white beard who appeared suddenly out of nowhere. He offered to help spin all the straw into solid gold threads in return for a simple bracelet her mother had given her as a token of her pride in her daughter for meeting the king. The king returned at sunrise and was pleasantly surprised by all the gold. The father, standing by his side, looked quite relieved.

The maiden thought that was the end of it and looked forward to becoming the new queen.

"No," said the king. "I have a bigger room with more straw for you to spin into gold. If you fail, you and your father will still be executed."

As was mentioned earlier, the greedy king had actually prepared *two* more rooms full of straw, but he did not want to upset the distraught lady too much by telling her about the third one. After all, she *did* already provide him with a room full of solid gold thread.

Again, the maiden wept and despaired to be comforted by the old man who, for the price of a copper ring the maiden had found on her way to the castle, spun the straw in the larger room to solid gold. Come the next morning, surprise, surprise, the king announced he was only going to marry the poor maiden after she had spun all the straw in the third and largest room in his castle into more gold, all to be done by sunrise the following morning. Otherwise, it would be, "Off with their heads!"

"Are you sure these are the good guys in this story, Mam?" queried Mary. Tom seemed to have had enough and was fast asleep, sucking contentedly on his thumb.

"Of course, dear. Wait till you hear what the old

man wants in return next… oh, shocking!"

The maiden sat in a room bigger than a football field, filled to the very last inch with straw. She did not cry in despair this time, as on cue, the strange little man arrived to offer his help. He sighed at the giant pile of straw. "He's really pushing it, isn't he?" said the old man. "Are you sure you want to be married to such a greedy gut?!"

"Yes, of course, it's what poor, kind maidens are *supposed* to do," said the poor, kind maiden.

Mary was shaking her head at this point.

Hence, the strange old man labored all night, spinning tonnes of straw into gold, while the maiden slept peacefully, dreaming about her upcoming royal wedding. The old man, a couple of minutes before sunrise, woke her up. He was utterly exhausted and requested his payment.

"I see you don't have any more nice trinkets to offer as my reward. Why don't we wait till you get married first, and as queen of all the lands, you can give me a nice present, then?" he offered.

"No, no. For all that you have done for me, I offer you my first-born son," promised the maiden.

"I don't think you should do that. I am quite sure you would grow very fond of your baby once he's born.

Why don't you just get me a woolly hat or something instead?"

"I will not hear of such absurdity! I am now a queen-to-be, and I will gladly make this sacrifice for your noble deed, sir."

"I don't *really* want another baby…"

Knock…

Knock…

Knock…

The man disappeared into thin air as the happy king stepped into the room and declared he would now deem the maiden fit to be his wife. He did not mention he had run out of straw, nor had he any more room to spare in his castle.

They got married that very afternoon in a simple ceremony, presided over by the castle priest and two witnesses: the maiden's overjoyed father and the king's rather envious brother. The dowry was a small box full of solid gold thread.

Mary made a gesture that she was about to get sick.

The maiden had never been happier. Exactly nine months later, a beautiful bouncing baby boy was born to the golden couple.

One night, the strange old man returned, looking rather sheepish.

"I told you he was evil, didn't I?!" said Mam.

Anyway, the old man asked for the gift that was promised.

The new queen sobbed and kicked about in despair at the thought of losing her baby.

"Look, my dear, why don't I just take him to live with us for a couple of days? Then I can bring him back…"

The queen tragically declared she could never be parted from her son for even a second and begged she be given another task in compensation.

The old man was getting quite fed up by this stage, so he said, "Just read my name out loud, and we'll call it even; it's written here on my name tag, starting with the letter R…"

The queen covered her eyes and cried, "Come back in three days and three nights, and if I cannot guess your secret name by then, you may take my prince." The old man sighed and went away.

The queen summoned all her knights and nobles, every page and messenger, to her throne room. The king, during this time, was counting all the gold threads; he was halfway through the first room.

The queen ordered her brave men and women to search far and wide, to go into every village and forest, and discover the name of the old man who so threatened her son. Hence, the great search began, where every house and hut, every field and wood, was turned upside down in order to carry out the queen's wishes.

The strange old man, meanwhile, waited in his tinker's cart just outside the palace gates, with a big sign at the side of the cart that read: *RUMPLESTILSKIN no job too big or too small*. But he was ignored by the hundreds of knights and nobles, who thundered past him on their powerful steeds for the next three days and three nights. Finally, as the appointed hour approached, the old man went home to his wife and told her the whole story.

"Why don't you build a great bonfire in the woods, dear, then dance around it like a madman and shout out your name at the top of your voice?" suggested his wife.

"Who would be *dumb* enough to fall for that?" said the old man, close to tears in despair.

"It had better work. I won't have a stinking, wailing baby in this house; seven children are seven too many!"

Seeing no other way, the old man did as his wife counseled, building the biggest bonfire the kingdom had ever known and screaming his name repeatedly at the top of his voice.

Now, who should happen to come upon him at that moment but none other than the queen's father, back from the city fair, having told anyone who would listen that his other daughter can turn glass into diamonds.

The old man saw the queen's father hiding behind a nearby tree, so he shouted his name even louder, even spelled it out as it was a very unusual name, over and over again:

R-U-M-P-L-E-S-T-I-L-S-K-I-N

R-U-M-P-L-E-S-T-I-L-S-K-I-N

R-U-M-P-L-E-...

Then, as the father crept silently away, Rumpelstiltskin, wanting to be absolutely certain, ran to him and gave his name tag to hand to the queen. Furthermore, he awaited several minutes before hastening to the castle gates, where he magically vanished and reappeared in the queen's bedroom, only to find that her father was just reading aloud the name on the tag to her.

With great hope, the old man asked, "So, my queen, what's my name?"

The queen looked to be thinking of a possible answer when the old man simply put out his hand for his name tag. The queen's father, in an act that fully redeemed his past failings, handed it back to him. Once it touched his palm, Rumpelstiltskin vanished for the final time, never to be seen again.

And everyone lived happily ever after...

The End.

***

"Hmmm," said Mary, fingers drumming her chin shrewdly. "Let me get this straight. Rumpelstiltskin single-handedly spun all that straw into gold, saved the queen and her father from being executed, and only asked for what had been promised him. I'd say he's the real hero in this story."

Tom seemed to nod slightly in agreement in his sleep.

"You certainly have a weird way of looking at things, my daughter."

"Not weird, just plain speaking. It is what it is!" Mary gave a satisfied grin and stood to get a biscuit from the cardboard.

"How do you spell Rumpelstiltskin again, Mam?"

There was no answer. Mary found the biscuit and walked back to rejoin Mam and Tom.

"Mam, didn't you hear me? I said how do you spell…"

Mam was lying next to Tom. She appeared to be in a trance, facing the ceiling with her eyes closed, her chest moving slowly with her breathing.

All of a sudden, Mary began to feel very queasy, a sharp pressure building up in her head, with pulsating red light blazing behind her eyes.

Knock…
Knock…
Knock…

CHAPTER 8
FOOL'S GOLD

A jumble of confusing images flashed inside Mary's brain.

First, of a man whom she somehow knew was her father, though she had never met him before, giving her a hug.

Then, of a little old man hopping off a wall and helping lost little girls and boys.

Next, of the same man grinding wheat into flour, flour which burst into the air and rained down as little loaves of bread.

The final vision was of the old man standing outside her door, a friendly smile on his face. A warm feeling blossomed in her heart. If Mary would just open the door and let him in, she, Mam, and Tom would live happily ever after.

So, Mary opened the door.

The figure outside looked grossly bloated. His dirty, grey beard stuck out like the quills on a hedgehog, his hands resembling a pig's trotters. His head was too big for his hat, which was hanging over one hairy ear.

Mary heard a loud, rumbling sound and guessed it came from the man's stomach. He looked ravenous, flecks of saliva dripping from his mouth into his bushy beard.

The Beastie leered at Mary and pointed his hooved hand at the biscuit she was still holding. She handed it to him without speaking.

"May I come in, Mary?" He spoke in a harsh, guttural voice. "We're supposed to be best friends now. I also know all about you. You like baking, and blue is your favorite color. Only best friends know that!"

He was breathing heavily, the rancid smell of wet fur wafting over Mary.

"All children love me! Let me come in, and we'll have a little party. Girls like parties."

Mary took a step back. The Beastie's jaws opened in a wide smile, displaying black, jagged teeth. He whooped and gave a little jig of joy, knocking the heels of his boots together in mid-air in anticipation of finally being able to come inside.

Then, just as he was about to cross the threshold,

some of the clouds in Mary's brain faded as if blown away by a gust of wind, and she remembered something. She was not allowed to talk to strangers and never let anyone inside her home.

Mary raised her right hand and cried, "No! Stop! Stop now! You're not allowed in!"

The Beastie's face contorted in fury. Through gritted teeth, he said in a low, menacing voice, "Little Mary, I'm your friend, remember? I make wishes come true. I got rid of all those bad people for you. You still have your third wish. I promised you that, and I always keep my promises! I can spin thread into gold, too, if you want!"

"What?! How do you know? I don't want another wish. I'm happy as I am. I don't need your fool's gold!"

Suddenly, at that precise moment, a large rat dashed behind the Beastie. Swift as a weasel, he grabbed it between his trotters and forced it, squealing, into his inner coat pocket next to the biscuit.

"What are you going to do to that rat?"

"Nothing! I just need a bit of company, that's all." He stroked the rat from the outside of his coat. "I like small animals and small children too. Would you like to come out and play with us?"

"No!" Mary said, cringing away, but the rat had

given her an idea. *Maybe this horrid man-beast will leave her family alone after this?*

She stood her ground and declared, "For my very final wish, I want you to make all the rats go away."

"Ahh… is that all? So easy, so very easy. That's all three wishes, my dear. I'll see you soon…" He licked his lips grotesquely and clacked his trotters together.

Mary closed the door.

"Time for another story, honey?" said Mam, sitting up beside Tom.

"Yes, please," said Mary, wondering where her biscuit went.

Chapter 9
Rat Pizza

"YUCK! This whole place stinks! Where's it coming from?"

Aunt Kay had just come in for a late breakfast with Mary and Mam. She looked under her boots and wiped them on the doormat.

"Sorry, I stepped on something wet out there. *Gross!"*

Mary had woken up that morning to the most awful smell imaginable. She had once come across a dead cat at the back of their building that had been lying there for days, its bloated body covered with flies and maggots. The smell was overpowering, but this was actually much worse. It was so bad that even Tom, who was not known to be the cleanest of babies, was in a foul mood and would not stop crying.

"I don't know, Kay," said Mam. "Maybe the drain

is blocked or something."

"There goes breakfast," said Aunt Kay, who looked like she was about to get sick. "Smells like something just died in here."

"Maybe it's the rats, Mam," said Mary all of a sudden. "Maybe they're dead, stuck behind the walls and under the floor, too." Both Mam and Aunt Kay stared at Mary.

"What made you say that?" asked Aunt Kay.

"I don't know."

"That could be it," said Mam. "Certainly smells like it. Don't get me wrong, I'm not too sorry if those fur balls go to Rat Heaven, but how did it happen?"

"Lightning, maybe?" said Aunt Kay. "I've heard a tale of lightning striking a building, and all the birds nesting in it just went zap... instant fried dinner!"

"Lightning? Was there a thunderstorm last night?"

"Who knows, with this weather we're having. You should call the landlord."

"The landlord? I haven't seen him in over three years! I wouldn't be surprised if he's under the floor with the dead rats."

"Mam! What an awful thing to say."

"Sorry, dear. This smell is giving me a dreadful headache."

"Let's go out then," said Aunt Kay, looking out at the window. The sky looked clear for once, the weak sunlight reflecting off the snow-covered rooftops.

"Let me put together some sandwiches," said Mam. "I haven't been out in ages."

Once everyone had donned their coats, gloves, and boots, they started down the steps.

"What's that?" said Mary, pointing.

They were halfway down, Tom in Mam's arms, his round face staring out from his furry bear onesie, when they came across a large stain on the wall.

Aunt Kay leaned in closer and inhaled sharply. "*BLLEEAGHH!*" She gagged and nearly vomited, her eyes watering. "That's where the smell is coming from!"

They stood back and stared at the dirty stain until they realized it was actually a rat, a very flat bloody mess, but still clearly a rat. It looked like somebody pummelled it with a large hammer, its pink-clawed hands and feet spread out like a starfish, its long tail forming an *S* shape on the wall.

"What happened to it?" said Mary, shuddering.

"Who cares? Let's go!" said Aunt Kay, who was beginning to get dizzy. Further on, they saw more of the squashed rats. They were everywhere, on the walls, stairs, landing, and even the ceiling, looking like gruesome thin-crust pizzas.

"Watch where you step," said Mam as they skipped over a giant puddle on the carpet, which was previously three very fat rats squashed together. "Didn't you see them when you came in this morning, Kay?"

"Ugh! There's something in my hair," said Aunt Kay. She looked up and saw a rat pizza still dripping blood and muck from the ceiling. A large wet piece of gunk fell and flopped onto the side of Aunt Kay's mouth. This time, she did get sick on the stairs before they were finally able to get out of the flat.

As soon as they burst out the door, Aunt Kay grabbed large handfuls of clean white snow and started rubbing them on her face and through her hair.

"Kay, stop that! You're creating a scene."

"Shut up, Ger! If you've got rat guts in *your* hair, you'd do the same."

There was nobody around that morning. Once Aunt Kay's face and hair were free from pieces of a dead rat, the four were on their way, relishing the fresh, clean air after the horrible suffocating stink of their building.

"That was just about the most disgusting thing ever! Looks like you guys are moving in with me until you get this sorted," said Aunt Kay.

"Thanks," said Mary. "But I think that mess will

go away soon."

"Who's going to clean that up? You've been saying very strange things lately, dear," said Aunt Kay. "Are you ok?"

Mary nodded. Mam exchanged a worried glance with her sister.

***

They wandered down the street, still in shock by what they had just experienced. Eventually, they found themselves standing outside Saint Mary's Cathedral, a grey, squat building with Roman pillars at the entrance. It towered over the surrounding buildings. The front door was shut, where thick piles of snow had accumulated over the months.

"They named that place after you," said Aunt Kay to Mary with a smile.

"Let's sit over here," said Mam, indicating a stout wooden bench on the pavement. Mary unpacked the remainder of the bread she had baked and a few slices of hard cheese.

They sat in silence for a while, feeling cold and miserable, chewing on their sandwiches. Mam broke off chunks of bread and fed it to Tom, which he spat out immediately, making a disgusted face. She tried again, but Tom refused to open his mouth and turned his head to the side, looking very annoyed indeed.

Aunt Kay reached out and pinched his cheek playfully. "Good thing you still can't talk, huh, little fella?"

"I don't think we should eat any more of this bread, Mam."

"Why? You just baked it yesterday."

"There's something wrong with the flour. While I was mixing it, it kind of smelled a bit funny."

"Has it expired?" asked Aunt Kay. "You should have said earlier."

"No, the date's fine. I'm sorry…"

"You're alright, honey. What with rats all over the place, we need to be extra careful what we put in our mouths. Here…" Aunt Kay took all the bread and scattered them at the base of a streetlamp next to the bench.

"I'm sure those skinny pigeons would be only too delighted."

Tom soon became restless and started bouncing on Mam's thighs, so they got up and walked further along. They eventually turned down a small side street heading towards O'Connell Street. Here, it grew much darker as the closed-set buildings blocked off the sun. Huge piles of snow had gathered outside shuttered doors, forcing them to walk in the middle of the road.

"I can't seem to shake that disgusting rat smell!" complained Aunt Kay suddenly. "Ger, do you see anything left in my hair?"

"It's not you, Kay," said Mam. She was staring up at the surrounding buildings. All the windows were closed except for one on their left side, one story up. A big sign read *Oriental Herbal Tea* on the window front below. As with the other buildings, it appeared long deserted.

They could see faint trails of smoke coming from the window, like someone was smoking or cooking inside. They heard a croaky male voice humming a tune inside.

"I think the smell is coming from there."

They stood transfixed, gazing up at the open window. Mary felt a strong sense of foreboding upon hearing the voice. A vague memory rocked inside her brain, an echo of something dangerous that threatened her and her family. She began to feel light-headed, her heart palpitating fast as cold sweat trickled down her spine.

"Let's turn back," whispered Aunt Kay.

"Why are we whispering?" whispered Mam.

Aunt Kay shivered. "Let's just go."

They hurried back to the relative brightness of

Marlborough Street and walked further until they reached Talbot's Street before anyone spoke. Soft snowflakes had started to fall.

"Gosh, what was that all about?" said Aunt Kay, looking quite pale. "I felt terrible back there. Did you guys feel it, too?"

Mam nodded, looking worried. "Who could be living in that place? And what was he cooking? It smelled dreadful."

Mary stood trembling, holding her tummy with both hands like she wanted to get sick. "Are you ok, honey?" Mam placed her hand on Mary's forehead.

Mary suddenly lurched to one side, and Aunt Kay grabbed her to keep her from falling. Her eyes began to close. The snow shower became heavier, the wind gaining the pace of a blizzard.

"We need to get her inside!" cried Mam. "We'll go to my place," said Aunt Kay.

"There's no time!"

They were standing in the middle of the empty street, surrounded on both sides by shops and flats. They started beating on every closed door and window they came to, shouting for help, their voices muffled by the emergent storm.

They came to a glazed oak door, hands already

sore and their throats hoarse from shouting. The brass knocker was in the form of a crescent moon. Aunt Kay knocked for all she was worth, with Mam holding onto both Tom and Mary.

As they were about to give up, they heard the sound of bolts being drawn back and a key being turned. The door cracked open. A face partly concealed by shadow peaked out.

"Please help us!" cried Aunt Kay immediately. "My niece is very sick!"

The door swung open. The face belonged to a tall, dark-skinned young man with a short beard. He wore a thick cotton robe and leather slippers, a white cloth hat over his thick, curly hair. He glanced quickly at the group, his dark eyes resting momentarily on Mary, who was close to collapsing, and Tom, who looked like a baby polar bear, except he was obviously freezing.

"Come in," the man said, then closed the door shut behind them against the blizzard. He pushed the bolts in place before turning the key in the lock.

CHAPTER 10
MARY'S WISHES

A sudden quiet came over the group. It was dark inside the building but not gloomy and mercifully warm. They faced a long flight of steps, at the top of which a soft light emanated.

"Please follow me," said the young man.

Aunt Kay took Tom from Mam, and together, they followed the man up the narrow steps. They came to a surprisingly spacious hall. There was no furniture. The whitewashed walls were hung with green tapestries decorated with wavy silver script. A large skylight dominated the roof, through which sunlight streamed through.

"What is this place?" asked Mam. They were standing just outside the hall.

"It's a mosque," said the man. "A place for prayer and meditation." He spoke with a pleasant, sing-song accent.

"Sorry, we didn't mean to disturb you."

"Not at all. As you can see, apart from myself, there's no one else here. My name is Ésa. I'm the caretaker here. Please come inside and rest while I make some tea."

Ésa disappeared up another flight of steps.

Mam was about to take a step inside when she noticed the thick, lush red carpet covering the whole floor.

"Should we take our boots off?"

"He didn't say," said Aunt Kay.

"Maybe we should anyway. We don't want to ruin the man's nice carpet."

They placed their wet boots upon a large wooden rack and stepped inside the room. They were greeted with the delicate scents of jasmine and lavender, and the lush carpet felt wonderful beneath their cold feet and tickled their toes.

Mary was starting to feel much better. She strolled away from the others towards the middle of the hall.

"You feeling ok, honey?"

Mary turned and nodded at her mother. She peered up at the skylight and saw dark clouds racing overhead, the snow pitter-pattering on the thick sheets of glass.

The others joined her, and they sat down on the

carpet.

"Well, this is nice," said Mam, leaning back and stretching out her legs. "I've never been inside a mosque before. I didn't even know we had one around here."

"I knew someone from Morocco once," said Aunt Kay. "He showed me these nice pictures of mosques from all over the world, with really tall minarets and huge domes. They don't have any chairs, though, do they?"

They were starting to feel very warm. Mam unzipped Tom's onesie, laid him down on the carpet, and gave him his bottle from the carrier bag. He happily sucked away, his eyes gradually starting to close. Mary placed her head down next to him.

"Your man seems nice," said Aunt Kay, gazing at the tapestries. "Seems very young to be caretaker, doesn't he? He looks to be what, eighteen?"

"The beard makes him look older. Don't you get any ideas, Kay. You're old enough to be his mother," Mam teased.

"No way he's that young. I bet you he's making us mint tea this very minute. They always make mint tea in Morocco."

Before her sister could respond, Ésa reappeared carrying a tray laden with a steaming metal teapot and tiny glasses, a plate of hard biscuits on the side. He, too, had removed his slippers before entering the prayer area.

"The babies are ok?" he asked. Both Tom and Mary were asleep, snoring softly.

"Yes, thank you," said Mam. "And thank you so much for helping us. We're very grateful. It was getting desperate out there."

"I would have let you in sooner, but you have to be careful these days. Food is scarce, and people would do anything to survive. Who can blame them?" said Ésa.

Aunt Kay took a sip from her glass.

"Sorry," said Ésa. "I ran out of milk."

"That's ok. This isn't mint tea."

"Mint tea?"

Mam flashed Aunt Kay a warning glare, which she promptly ignored.

"You're not from Morocco?"

"No, I'm from Burkina Faso."

"Bikini-what-so?"

"It's in Western Africa."

"Ah, I see. What tea is this, then?"

"Barry's tea."

"Barry's? But we're in Dublin, mate."

"Sorry?"

"That's ok, Ésa," interjected Mam, eyes sending daggers towards Aunt Kay's deceptively innocent face.

"We're really very grateful for the hospitality. Won't you join us?"

"Sure," said Ésa. He took a glass, murmuring something under his breath before taking a sip.

"Sorry, what did you say?" asked Aunt Kay.

"I didn't say anything," said Ésa.

"No, you said something before you drank your tea."

"Oh, I said *Bismillah*. It's just a habit of mine."

"What does it mean?"

"It's a sort of prayer in my language, asking for blessings. If you say it, no evil spirit would disturb your meals."

"Evil spirits drink tea?"

"*Kayyy...*"

"Well, they can take away the spiritual goodness from your food and drink. Anyway, you're most welcome to stay the night. I have extra pillows and sleeping bags."

"No, thank you, we don't want to intrude," said Mam. "We'll leave when the storm stops."

"Who knows how long it would last? I'll bring the stuff down anyway, and you can decide later what you want to do."

Ésa took hold of their tray and stood to go.

Mary suddenly awoke and looked up at him.

"Wait. If I say *Bismillah* before I sleep, will it also stop evil spirits from scaring me?"

Mam reached out and stroked her hair. "She's been having really bad nightmares lately."

Ésa sat back down in front of Mary, his dark eyes staring unblinkingly at her. "I'm sorry to hear it, Mary. It must be scary then to go to sleep."

"But she'll grow out of it, won't she?" said Aunt Kay.

"I don't…"

"How do you make them stop?" Mary implored, eyes glistening.

Ésa looked away, remaining silent. Tom stirred in his sleep, his hands clutched into tight fists in front of him.

"Tell me about the nightmares."

"I don't remember them when I wake up. But I know something bad happens when I sleep. When I close my eyes, I feel something is there, waiting to hurt me."

"Honey, I didn't know they were that bad." Mam shuffled closer, putting her arm around Mary.

"Wait," said Aunt Kay. "Is anyone actually hurting you, girl? Anyone in your building?" She exchanged a worried glance with Mam.

"No!" cried Mary, covering her face. "There's no

one." Tom awoke and started crying. Ésa picked him up and hugged him to his chest. Tom placed his cheek on Ésa's chest and began dozing off.

"It's all right. Nothing bad is gonna happen to you here, God Willing. I'll tell you one thing. Back home, when I was little, my mother used to get me to wash my feet before I go to bed. She said if I sleep with dirty feet, I'll get bad dreams."

"Really?" asked Aunt Kay, staring at Ésa's feet as he paced up and down the hall, Tom in his arms.

"Well, I don't believe it now," said Ésa awkwardly, unable to hide his feet. "But I've kept up the habit, so I can't sleep without washing my feet first!"

The young man left them to the privacy and comfort of the prayer hall for long periods of the day. They washed in a nearby room where there were marble seats and taps running warm water. He brought more tea and biscuits down to them, eyeing Aunt Kay suspiciously whenever she glanced at his feet.

Later that afternoon, they heard Ésa busily preparing a meal in the kitchen upstairs. A delicious smell of cooking wafted down to them, making their mouths water and stomachs rumble. Mam fretted constantly whether they should offer to help while Aunt Kay explored the hall. She slid open the door of a long cupboard built into the wall, containing what looked like colorful rosary beads and thick books arranged neatly upon rows of shelves. She also sniffed some scented oil contained in small glass jars, marveling at the variety of their fragrances. She decided to place a drop of what smelled like rose oil on her left wrist.

They later shared a simple meal of long-grained rice fried in olive oil and spices, boiled eggs sprinkled with salt and white pepper, and flava beans cooked with onions and tomatoes, all washed down with ice-cold water. Ésa apologized for being unable to offer anything else, but they said it was one of the best meals they had had in a long time.

As it turned out, the storm raged on for the rest of the day into the evening, the wind howling loudly and shaking the shutters of the skyline.

They ended up staying the night, sleeping together in the middle of the carpeted floor. Mary excused herself to go to the washroom before turning in and washed her feet, wriggling her tiny toes in warm tap water. She snuggled close to Tom and wrapped her arm around him. "*Bismillah,* Tom," she whispered and kissed his cheek.

Without realizing it, they all dreamed the same dream, even Tom. They were lying together in a field of soft grass, surrounded by bushes of sweet-scented red and yellow roses. The sun was warm on their faces, with the sound of sheep bleating softly from a nearby field.

***

Mary awoke sometime in the night, Mam and Tom on her right, Aunt Kay on her left, all wrapped snugly in warm sleeping bags.

She gazed up at the night sky through the skyline. The rolling clouds were gone, replaced by twinkling blue and green stars. One of these bright jewels was streaking across the velvet sky, starting from one edge of the of the skyline, zooming towards the center.

Mary followed its path with her eyes and wondered for an instant if it would crash into the other stars. It did not, of course, and continued on its space journey until it was right in the middle of her vision. Then, a very peculiar thing happened: the shooting star slowed and stopped altogether! Mary blinked her eyes a few times in disbelief, but there it was, a large diamond sparkling right in front of her.

A fuzzy feeling of warmth came over Mary, starting in her chest and spreading to her fingers, toes and head. All the pent-up fears and anxiety of the past few days quickly went away, and she felt completely relaxed. She thought of a wish before closing her eyes. She wished for safety and happiness for Mam, Tom, and Aunt Kay. She also wished for all the children, the cats and dogs that had gone missing, for the kind young man who helped them, and finally, she wished for herself.

Mary slowly opened her eyes, and now she was flying across the vast expanse of the universe, riding the shooting star as it continued on its voyage. Mary looked down upon a blue planet with an emerald island shining in a far corner. She lifted both her arms and felt the rhythm of the stars as they sparkled and shimmered.

Then she saw beings of immense light filling the spaces between the stars, whose faces and voices were of such beauty that she cried tears of joy. Three of these beings were carrying something protectively in their arms: Mary's precious wishes. They soared on indescribable wings, up and up, until they were lost to view in the vast cosmos.

As true slumber finally took over, Mary glimpsed a large crack that had appeared in the brick wall in her mind, the wall behind which the Beastie hid. Somewhere in the darkness, a man with the shadow of a swine screamed in rage, and suddenly Mary remembered everything.

CHAPTER 11
A PARTING GIFT

The dawn sun filtered through the sunroof, warm and soft on Mary's face as she awoke, hearing the comforting snores of Mam and Aunt Kay.

Mary slowly inhaled, enjoying the peace and tranquillity of the moment. She opened her eyes to find a chubby, pink face staring upside down at her. Tom was already awake, sitting above her head. He smiled and slowly poked a wet finger into her eye.

"*Ouch!!*"

Tom crawled from one end of the hall to the other, looking back and screaming ecstatically as Mary chased after him.

Eventually, everyone got up and washed. Ésa served a delicious breakfast of warm flatbread spread with butter and honey and steaming black coffee.

"Are you a tea or coffee lover, Ésa?" inquired Aunt

Kay.

"I'd drink anything. Sorry, do you want me to get you some tea instead?"

"We're just fine, Ésa," interjected Mam. "Kay here can drink anything as well."

"How old are you, by the way?" inquired Aunt Kay.

"*Kayyy!*"

"I'm fifteen."

"Egad! I *am* old enough to be your mother."

"Come again?"

"Never mind, Ésa," said Mam. "I really think we should be going now."

Soon, they were plodding down the narrow flight of steps, their footsteps echoing in the narrow hall.

"Come in for a chat whenever you're passing by. You're just down the road from here," said Ésa at the door. Seagulls and crows greeted them as they stepped out onto the street. A fresh carpet of snow lay on the street, halfway covering their boots.

"Will do," said Aunt Kay, carrying Tom, who was testing his voice against the caws of the birds.

"Thank you so much, Ésa," said Mam. "Do please come over to our place sometime. You know where we are now. Little Mary here is a great baker."

"Will do."

Ésa leaned down so his face was level with Mary's, their dark brown eyes strikingly similar.

"My mother's name is Maryam. It's Arabic, which translates to…"

"… Mary," said Mary.

He said softly to her, "Did you sleep well last night?" to which Mary nodded. "No more bad dreams?" and she shook her head.

Then Ésa whispered so quietly that only Mary could hear, "Whenever you need me, little Mary, I'll be there, *inshaAllah*." He placed a tiny glass bottle filled with a dark golden liquid in her hand as a parting gift, which she carefully placed in her pocket.

They walked back up Talbot's Street and turned the corner into Marlborough Street, heading towards their flat. They gave the side street from yesterday a wide berth, but somehow, it did not seem as sinister as before. All the windows were closed shut, and the air smelled clean and pure.

"What was that he said?" Aunt Kay asked Mary, who just smiled in reply.

I'm not going to be afraid anymore!

***

They approached the flat, covering their noses, cringing

in anticipation of the stink and mess from the dead rats. But as Mary had said, there were no more stains and puddles as they entered the corridor on the ground floor. The carpets, steps, and walls were all free from the mucky stains. Still, Aunt Kay covered her hair with both hands and avoided looking up until they were safely back in their apartment.

"When I said those steps would be the death of me, I didn't expect it would involve avoiding minced mice."

"You're being very quiet, Mary," said Mam. "Are you sure you're ok?"

Mary was sitting on the couch next to Aunt Kay, with Mam sitting across in her favorite armchair.

"Mam," Mary began, her young face frowning. "He was here."

"Who was here, Luv? What are you talking about?"

Mary looked her mother straight in the eye, her voice steady.

"That evil man who's been taking kids away. He was here."

Aunt Kay, who was sipping hot coffee, spluttered and spilled her cup. "What?! When?!"

"He's been here three times already. He was here two nights ago. He knocked on the door, but I wouldn't let him in. He'll be back again tonight."

"You're scaring the *bejeebers* out of me, girl! Stop talking like this," said Aunt Kay.

Mam came and knelt in front of Mary, cupping her little face gently with her hand. She held her daughter's gaze and saw only truth in her deep brown eyes.

"Tell me everything, Luv. Start from the beginning. Leave nothing out." Thus, Mary told her mother everything.

***

"And you're saying, each time he was here, I go into some sort of magical trance?" said Mam.

"Yes!" said Mary.

"And I'd forget everything afterwards?" Mam looked bewildered.

"Maybe it's like PTSD," volunteered Aunt Kay. "I've heard about this. People lose their memory when they've experienced something really bad."

Mam glanced at Aunt Kay before saying, "Did he ever hurt you?"

"No Mam, he's never touched me. But I think he wants to. I think he needs my permission before he can do anything to me."

"How is it that you remember now, Luv?" said Mam, her gaze not leaving Mary's face.

"I'm not sure... but last night, I made a wish,

asking for help, because I was feeling so confused. There was something in my head, like a big wall, it hurts my brain, and I wished for it to go away."

"What do we do?" said Aunt Kay.

"We can let the Guards know," said Mam.

"And say what, that Rumpelstiltskin is paying us a visit?"

"Well, we'll have to change the story a bit. We'll say an intruder or robber has been here. You'll know what to say, Kay, when you see them."

"Ok, ok, but with so many kids missing already, they don't seem to be able to stop this monster."

"They won't be able to stop him," said Mary. "We have to fight him a different way."

"How?!" said Mama and Aunt Kay together.

"I don't know yet, but somehow I know he'll be here again, and he'll talk to me, and I just have to figure out how to stop him."

"That's crazy," said Aunt Kay, standing up now and walking around the living room. "Look... I'll pack some stuff and stay here with you tonight. We'll put extra locks, and... and..."

"... and we'll have a water spray. No, a bucket of water that you throw over us to wake us up if he shows up. But you're not going to open the door, anyway.

And… "

"You'll have your rolling pin ready."

"Yes, my *Mickey Masher*!"

"And I'll bring my taser gun, so if he dares show his ugly face here, I'll shock his butt off!"

So, the trio spent the rest of that day planning on how to tackle the wicked man when he returns. Aunt Kay went out that afternoon and walked all the way to the police station. The haggard-looking Guard listened sympathetically and reassured her they would increase their surveillance of the area, which was already under close monitoring since the last missing child. Next, she packed her clothes, toiletries, and tools they would need to put on an extra lock.

Finally, with her fully charged taser gun in her bag, Aunt Kay went back up to the apartment, getting ready to kick Rumpelstiltskin's butt.

CHAPTER 12
MORE BEAST THAN MAN

Knock…
Knock…
Knock…

"You're *not* allowed in!" said Mary firmly.

She was standing on her stool, peering through the peephole. This evening, the Beastie appeared taller. Somehow, he stood at the same level as her on the opposite side, his huge green eye gazing back. *Did he have a stool to stand on, too?*

"What? But I thought we were friends? I know your name, your favorite color, your favorite song. I even got you flour because you love baking. I also went *Stomp! Stomp! Stomp!* all over your walls and roof, squashing all the nasty rats for you."

Mam and Aunt Kay were staring blankly at the wall, dripping wet from the bucket of water Mary had just thrown over them, Tom lying soundless on the bed.

The Beastie stepped back from the peephole, and Mary noticed that not only was he taller, but his face had changed again: his nose was a snout, and the lower part of his face resembled a bearded hog. From what little she could see, it seemed his legs were longer, and his hands were hairy paws.

He then bent down on all fours and started running in circles outside her door, grunting loudly. This went on for several minutes before he stopped outside her door again.

Knock…

Knock…

Knock…

This time, the knocking was followed by a sniffling and scratching sound.

Scratch…

Scratch…

Scratch…

A sound an animal would make if it wanted to come inside. His face appeared once more at the peephole. It was back to his previous one, that of an old man with a long, hooked nose and dirty grey beard.

"Why don't you just open the door and I'll give you a nice surprise! You'd like that!"

"You're not allowed in!"

The doorknob started to turn and rattle violently.

"LET ME IN! LET ME IN!" he roared, his voice more beast than man.

"No!" shouted Mary back. "Go away! Leave my family alone!"

Then, the Beastie seemed to relax again. He smiled through the peephole, a sly smile, and spoke in a gentle voice: "Did you like what I did to those plump little rats? *Stomp! Stomp! Stomp!* I'd never had so much joy! That was a really *fun* wish you made. Make another one, a fourth one, a bonus wish from your *bestest* friend! You're such a kind, pretty girl. I would be very sad if I left without granting you an extra wish!"

"I wish for you to go far away!"

The Beastie gave a fierce growl and slammed his head against the door, rattling the hinges. Over and over again, he yanked his head back and headbutted the door, howling like a mad dog.

Then, just as quickly, he calmed down again and said, "No, my dear, that's not how wishes work. Wish for something nice, a diamond ring, a singing bird, or a box of delicious chocolates! You like chocolates, don't you, Mary? Just open the door…"

"Go away!"

The soft voice turned beastly again. "You're being a bad girl, Mary, a very bad girl. You should be punished. I'm going to rip you with these claws, chew your fingers and toes, and boil your fluttering heart!"

The Beastie suddenly became quiet.

Mary, who was shaking like a leaf, tip-toed to her side of the door and placed her left ear against it.

Then came the sound of him weeping. "All I ever wanted was to make people happy. I don't have any friends. No one likes me. Nobody gives me any presents. *Boo Hoo Hoo…* poor, lonely me…"

Mary, who always had a kind heart, felt pity for the creature but remained silent.

Sniff, sniff. The Beastie cried outside the door for long minutes. He then seemed to compose himself and said, "Will you give me something, Mary? Just give me a small gift, a present, and I'll go far, far away, and not bother you ever again, I promise!"

"What do you want?" asked Mary tentatively. "I won't open this door!" She peeped through the peephole and saw a huge, teary green eye staring back at her.

"No… no… don't open this door, Mary. Just give me your favorite thing, something that you like very much, so that I may cherish it, too. Then I will go from here, I swear!"

"I don't have anything…"

"Everyone has a favorite thing, a toy, a book…"

Mary pictured her favorite little red apron. The thought of losing it to this creature, this beast of a man, pained her. *But, if it would make him go away…*

"Ok, I'll give you my red apron, but how can I give it to you without opening this door?"

The Beastie rubbed his paws in glee. "Just repeat this phrase after me, dearie. I told you I'm very special! Just say: I give to you my most *favorite* thing."

"Then you'll go away? Promise?"

"I promise!"

Mary said the words, "I give to you my most favorite thing," and watched as the Beastie walked away, whistling a merry tune.

CHAPTER 13
BIG SISTER

"*Ugh*! I'm soaking wet!!" A disgusted Aunt Kay looked down at herself.

"So am I! What happened?" Mam then caught the haunted look in her daughter's eyes.

"He was here."

"What?" cried both adults together.

"But it's ok, I took care of it. He promised to go away if I gave him my apron, my favorite thing, to remember me by."

"But, honey," said Mam. "You're wearing your apron now."

Mary looked down in horror at the red piece of cloth around her waist. It had the words *Favorite Sister* stitched on it.

"Wait!" Mam shouted in sudden panic. "Where's Tom?!!"

"He was sleeping on the bed, wasn't he?" said Aunt Kay, voice trembling. They both rushed to the bed and threw open the covers. They searched frantically in every part of the apartment: under the bed, behind it, in the closet, in the bathroom, everywhere.

Mary could only stare numbly as the terrible realization struck her. Her most favorite thing, the one thing she loved the most above everything else, with all her heart, wasn't the apron, nor anything like it; it was her baby brother. She had given her precious baby brother to that monster…

After checking under the bed for the third time, Aunt Fay said, "I'll go check outside. Maybe he'd crawled…"

"No, Tom's gone. That man's taken him. He was here. He tricked me," Mary's voice cracked with suppressed terror.

"What? He was *in* here?" cried Mam, eyes wide with alarm and disbelief.

"I didn't let him in. He was outside. He cast a spell on you again. I told him to go away many times…" Mary took a big shuddering breath. "He said he'd go away, leave us alone if I gave him my most favorite thing. I wanted to give my apron. But he took Tom instead." Mary started crying.

"Let's go after them, then!" Aunt Kay burst into action, pulling on her boots.

"The Guards!?" said Mam, now visibly trembling.

"*I'll* get them," said Aunt Kay. "While you…"

"I know where he's taken Tom!" cried Mary, jumping up suddenly. "We need to go there, now!"

Without bothering to explain, Mary ran out and flew down the stairs, still in her apron. The rest grabbed their coats, Mam snatching Mary's from the hanger and the rolling pin. Aunt Kay had the taser gun in her bag. Together, they dashed down the steps and out the front door after Mary. They saw her already far ahead, running full pelt down the street, making tiny footprints in the deep snow.

They caught up with Mary just as she passed the cathedral. She sprinted down the side street and stopped under the window that had previously spooked them, now shuttered closed, and dark as the rest. Dark clouds obscured the moon and stars, and the dim light from the streetlamps cast eerie shadows upon the walls.

"Tom's up there." Mary pointed up at the window while Mam placed her coat over her shoulders.

"How do we get in?" said Mam.

The bottom part of the shop, including the front door, was enclosed behind a steel shutter. The only possible access was via the windows on the first floor. Aunt Kay tried heaving the shutter open, but it was locked securely.

"Are you sure they're in there?" Aunt Kay said to Mary. "Maybe we should get the Guards now while..."

"Over here," said Mary. She went down a dark, narrow alley along one side of the building, Mam and Aunt Kay close behind her. They hurried in a single file to the back of the building. Even in the gloom, they could make out huge piles of rubbish: broken furniture, shattered glass amongst overflowing bins, and black plastic bags bursting with sludge. They also saw deep footprints in the snow, prints made by huge boots.

They stared at the building. There was no door, just an empty doorway, pitch black, which radiated a sinister aura.

"Wait!" Aunt Kay fumbled in her bag and found her cigarette lighter. "I knew you'd be useful someday," she murmured. Two clicks and a small flame burst forth, casting a circular light on the ground around them. "I can't see any more prints," said Aunt Kay, searching just outside the doorway. "What if they didn't go in here?"

"They did," insisted Mary. "I can feel it. I... I can also *see* them... in my brain." She pointed to her forehead, her small face raised, eyes pleading for the grownups to accept her words.

Mam looked at her daughter, red-rimmed eyes desperate to know. "Is Tom...?"

"I... I'm not sure, Mam... I think he's still ok..."

Then Mary pointed to the snow near the doorway, clear of any prints. "Remember the squished rats? The Beastie can walk on walls and ceilings, too."

"Is that the monster's name, *Beastie*?" asked Aunt Kay.

Before Mary could answer, a sudden sharp cry pierced the night, which was gone in an instant. "Let's go in," urged Mam. "*Please, God*," she murmured. "*Please keep my baby safe.*"

Together, they stood at the door's threshold, allowing their eyes to adjust to the near darkness. They began to see vague shapes, boxes, and rusted appliances scattered across the floor.

Mam held aloft her rolling pin and entered. "Let's stick close together," she said. Mary came next, Aunt Kay taking the rear, lighter held aloft in one hand, taser gun out and ready in the other. An unpleasant smell of rot and decay permeated the room.

"*Ouch!*" said Aunt Kay, the lighter going out. "Burnt my fingers." She clicked it back on. She thrust her arm to the ceiling, where empty light sockets were covered with thick layers of cobwebs.

They passed quickly through and went through another doorway into what appeared to be a windowless storehouse, the floor of which was a carpet of dust that had gathered over the years, causing them to cough and wipe their eyes. More cobwebs coated every corner; black hairy spiders scuttled away from the sudden intrusion of the light. They could just make out the outlines of a flight of steps leading to the floor above at the far corner. "Over there," pointed Mary.

The tiny flame of the lighter guttered again, then went out completely. Aunt Kay clicked it furiously many times, cursing under her breath, but to no avail. "Darn it," she said, throwing the empty lighter away. The three huddled closer together as the oppressive darkness enveloped them. Mary could not see her Mam standing right in front of her. "Stay close to me," whispered Aunt Kay in her ear.

They took small, cautious steps forward in the general direction of the stairs, their boots scuffling against unseen objects on the floor. Mam held the rolling pin out in both hands like a sword, waving it about side to side.

Squelch! Aunt Kay made a face in the darkness as she stepped on something soft and squishy. Mary clung on tightly to the back of Mam's coat. Her heart was hammering fast against her chest, and her palms felt sweaty. She forced herself to take deep breaths and focused on placing one foot in front of the other. Even sandwiched between Mam and Aunt Kay, she had never felt so afraid and so alone in all her life.

In that moment, in total darkness, Mary closed her eyes and prayed. She prayed with all her heart that her most favorite thing in the whole wide world was safe. She prayed he was not scared in the clutches of that monster. *"We're coming, Tom. Your big sister is here. I'll rescue you, and Mam will punish that horrid little man for taking you away, for frightening you so. Hang on tight, my love. Mary's coming!"*

Mam's rolling pin hit against something solid with a loud clunk. She reached out and grabbed the steel stair railing. As she went to take the first step up, she cried out in shock as her foot found empty space. She clutched at the railing to keep herself from falling, losing her hold of the rolling pin, which fell and crashed somewhere far below them.

"Are you ok, Ger?" said Aunt Kay from behind.

"I don't understand; where did the stairs go?" said Mam. She cautiously used her right foot to feel about in front of her and found steps which went *downwards* instead of going up.

"The steps, they lead down," said Mam. The sound of someone chuckling could be heard faintly, as if coming up from a deep well.

"We have to go down, Mam," said Mary. "They're down there, below us now."

"What dark illusion is this? God help us," murmured Mam. She placed her boot on the first step, holding on to the rail, then another, followed by Mary and Aunt Kay. The stairs went in a spiral, spinning anti-clockwise, plunging further underground.

At first, their progress was agonizingly slow, as one false step could cause them to fall crashing down in the pitch black.

"How deep does this go?" grumbled Aunt Kay. It felt like they had been climbing down for ages, their boots echoing off the steel steps. Fear for Tom, fear of this evil entity attacking them in the dark, gnawed at them with every step.

Finally, as the trio started to lose hope, a faint light appeared from beneath them, which grew brighter the further down they went. They made better progress; their steps were more confident as they were able to make out each individual step. The walls of the tunnel were made of concrete with a coating of moss, which felt damp under their fingers.

At last, they reached the bottom, their boots crunching on wet, muddy earth. They faced a closed wooden door from which light trickled out from its edges.

Mary placed her hand on the door. "Tom's in here," she breathed, and without looking back, she pushed the door open.

CHAPTER 14
RAGE & RELIEF

Mary, with Mam and Aunt Kay in tow, stepped into the Beastie's lair.

At first, it appeared to be another windowless warehouse, the ceiling too high to see without craning up their necks. A hot draught felt unpleasant on their skin after the chill of the staircase, the heat running over them in waves.

The reek of the place was overwhelming, causing them to cough and cover their noses with their coat sleeves. As their eyes slowly took in the surroundings, the true horror of the place assaulted their minds.

Bits of small bones and animal hide lay strewn across the dirt floor. Most terrible of all were the cages and what they contained. A long row of rusty metal cages lined the walls to their left and right. Each cage contained a child who stared at the newcomers with scared, hopeless eyes. As one, they surged forward to grip the bars and reached out with spindly arms, wailing and crying for help, their cages hardly big enough for them to stand upright.

Mary noticed that most of the boys and girls were younger than her, their long fingernails visible as they clawed the air in desperation through the bars.

"Dear God," whispered Mam, eyes wet with tears of grief.

The only thing that kept them standing on their shaky legs was the sight of a baby boy with brown curls, busily sucking on his big toe. He was lying on his back on what appeared to be a large pile of furry scarves.

Tom was also filthy. He was covered head to toe in wet muck and grime. Next to him, busily slicing a carrot into a big, black pot, boiling on top of a low stove, was the Beastie himself. He was standing on a stool very much like the one Mary had stood on as she peeked through the peephole at her apartment. He had his back to them and seemed oblivious to their arrival, crooning a little tune as smoke and steam wafted up through his bushy beard up to the ceiling, from where, of all things, a chandelier was giving off light.

"Tom!" screamed Mam as she, Mary, and Aunt Kay, as one, rushed across the room, their boots splashing in the red, brown goo. The Beastie turned his head and smiled at them, then continued preparing his stew.

Rage and relief both flickered simultaneously in Mary's heart. Rage at this man, this *beast*, for causing so much suffering and pain; relief that her baby brother looked unharmed from this distance. She clenched her fists as she raced through the slimy muck, now not ten pieces away, with Mam on her right screaming incoherently, Aunt Kay on her left, pointing her taser gun out like, well, a gun. They slipped and skidded but only had eyes for this terrible creature and their precious bundle.

The Beastie finished cutting up his carrot, inhaled the stew's spiced odor in satisfaction, then jumped and turned in mid-air to face them. As soon as his big boots splashed down, he clicked his fingers, and the three suddenly froze in mid-stride, agonizingly a few paces away from reaching Tom.

It was both very weird and disturbing at the same time to freeze like that. It reminded Mary of a game of musical chairs she had taken part in a long time ago when the music stopped, and you had to freeze. Otherwise, you're out of the game. The only thing was, this was not a game. The Beastie gave a chuckle that sounded like both the snort of a pig and bleat of a goat.

By the light of the chandelier, they had their first good view of the Beastie. His face was that of a nightmare, with the snout of a pig on a wide visage and long fangs protruding upwards from his lower jaw, which was covered by a long, dirty beard. Staring at them were the lifeless eyes of a goat with horizontal black pupils on yellow irises. Two short, curved horns protruded from the sides of his forehead. He was bare-chested, thick black fur matting his torso, and he wore dark green trousers above black chunky boots. Even from where they stood frozen, they could smell the wet animal stink from his body.

For Mam and Aunt Kay, this was their first time seeing this Beastie from hell, and the horror was clearly etched on their frozen faces. Mary kept her eyes staring boldly ahead, her young face screwed up in defiance, ears pricked up for any sound from Tom.

The Beastie stooped and lifted up Tom, dangling him, head down by one of his legs in front of them. His hands resembled that of a large ape with black inch-long claws. "So glad you could join me for some supper," he sneered. Tom started howling miserably.

"I thought I would only have starters, but now I'd have a three-course meal." He eyed Mary cruelly and plopped poor Tom down at their feet.

"Struggle as you like," he said, as tears and sweat trickled down their faces. "How stupendously silly of you to come and face me here, in my own domain?" He took out his sharp little knife and looked at his reflection in the pointed blade, delicately holding its bone handle with his taloned fingers. "Attack *me*?" He gave another chuckle.

"With this knife, I have carved many delicacies throughout the centuries. *Aah*, such fond memories…" he reminisced, starting to walk in a circle around them. "I stole it, of course, swiped it from the table of the last High King of Ireland while they were all sleeping soundly in their beds."

He sniggered, yellow eyes gazing into the distant past, and continued his monologue. "My dear Majesty, if you only knew what else I took from you… yes… such delightful memories."

The Beastie stopped in front of Mary; their heads levelled. "At the end of the day, it's only our memories, souvenirs from our past, that keep us company, isn't that so, little Mary?" He brought his face so close to hers that his wet snout was touching hers, goat eyes staring coldly, promising cruelty beyond measure. She had to inhale his rancid, meaty breath and almost puked in her closed mouth.

"You, my dear, have caused me so much trouble, you know that? All I wanted was to be your friend, didn't I? I was better than a friend, better than any father, to think of it. I granted you wishes and got rid of all the nasty rats and nastier people from your home. I gave you my own special flour and even remembered your favorite color. No friend would ever do these for you. And all I wanted was to come inside and play."

He gestured wide with his hairy upper limbs towards the cages. "Just look at all the other boys and girls here, little Mary. They let me in. They offered me friendship. They gave me what they loved most. All the good boys and girls, bless them all. They never refused me, Mary."

The Beastie reached out and patted her head. His hairy hand felt as cold as ice through her hair. "But you, my girl, why did you say no to me? What's going on inside that little head of yours?" He suddenly made a fist and rapped her head hard with his knuckles. "We'll soon find out now, won't we?" he said, coldly.

Mary blinked from the pain but continued to stare at the vile creature in front of her. She knew she should be very afraid. This was beyond her worst nightmare. She would likely not live to see the morning. But the sound of Tom's anguish cries from the floor fuelled her resolve;

having her Mam and Aunt at her side lent her strength. She remained calm and kept her unflinching gaze from leaving his. She refused to give this Beastie, this pathetic bully, the satisfaction of seeing her fear.

"Bismillah… Bismillah… Bismillah…"

"What are you mumbling?" The Beastie leaned in close and placed his pointed ear close to her mouth when he noticed Mary muttering under her breath.

"Are you saying sorry for being such a naughty, naughty girl? Come on, speak louder!"

Mary could see he was getting annoyed; this was not what he was expecting. She continued her mantra under her breath, glaring boldly at the Beastie. He pressed the tip of his knife on her cheek, drawing a drop of blood. "Tongue-tied?" He chortled, placing the knife point close to her eye. "Maybe this will help loosen it for you."

The Beastie suddenly licked the blood from the blade and snapped his furry fingers. Mary at once felt a lightening sensation across her face and throat as if an iron grip had been slackened, allowing her to move her head and neck. She looked up and saw that Mam and Aunt Kay were also partially released.

"Now, what was it you were going to say, my pretty? Oh, I must say, I do so love that lovely little apron you're wearing. *Favorite Sister! Ooh La La!* A sister that didn't care about her baby brother! Gave him away just like that!! *Terrible Sister* is more like it!!"

"No!! You tricked me…!"

"You *wanted* to be tricked. You wanted to give him away so you could have mammy all to yourself. All to your selfish self!"

Hot tears pricked like needles in Mary's eyes, falling down and stinging the wound on her cheek, but she could not wipe them away. She knew he was playing with her, using her love for Tom to torment her. Yet it still hurt to hear the words.

"Don't listen to him, Mary!" cried Mam beside her.

"Yeah!" chipped in Aunt Kay. "He's nothing but a *bully*; an ugly, SMELLY, STINKY…"

"*SILENCE!*" the Beastie shouted in Aunt Kay's direction.

"…MANGY, FILTHY, HAIRY…"

"*SHUT UP!!!*" He roared in her face.

"…lonely…" Mary finished softly.

"What did you say?" said the Beastie, looking back at Mary. This last description took the ancient monster completely by surprise that for long moments, he stood transfixed, eyebrows raised above his bulging orbits in confusion, his furry hand, which gripped the knife, trembling violently.

"You're lonely."

Mary looked at the Beastie with a mixture of wonder and sorrow. Their eyes met, her soft brown against his cruel yellow irises. Ever since her dream of flying amongst the stars, of seeing her wishes carried high into the heavens, as the wall in her head cracked and disintegrated, Mary had begun to *see*. Truly see, as the veil between human consciousness and reality was lifted. Without realizing it, since the night spent under the skylight, Mary had begun developing an affinity for this monster, an inner instinct to sense his whereabouts and empathize with his emotions.

Standing in front of her was the grotesque monster that was the Beastie, yet in her mind's eye, peeking timidly from behind a wall of iron, Mary saw the shadow of a scrawny little boy.

The Beastie took a step back, then another, away from where the three were standing, still magically petrified from the neck down. Tom, mercifully, had stopped crying but was lying motionless on the wet ground, eyes closed.

The Beastie seemed to be looking straight through them, his eyes unfocused, an indescribable look on his face. He seemed to be on the verge of remembering something, a fading echo from a long time ago. He reached out with his left hand and appeared to be pushing against an invisible wall. Then his face melted.

CHAPTER 15
YOU PROMISED

The Beastie's face melted and transformed in front of their eyes; his snout shrank into a hooked nose, his fangs disappeared behind a beardy mouth, his horns receded into a mat of hair, and his lifeless yellow irises darkened into green.

"Hey! Piggy! What's wrong with you? You sleep-walking or something?" called out Aunt Kay.

The Beastie looked at her with a blank expression for a few moments as if seeing her for the first time. His eyes then hardened, taking on their familiar brutish mien. He shook his head violently and pummelled it with his palm as if trying to knock a buzzing bee from out his pointy ear. He glared menacingly at each of them in turn, nostrils flaring wide. He paused at Mary and pointed a finger at her small face. Without the fur, she could see his hands appeared like that of an old man's, with gold rings shining brilliantly on every finger.

"You! What did you do to me? You little witch!!"

"It's time for you to let us go, now."

"What??!"

"Stop this evil thing and free us. We want to go home, now!"

The Beastie flung his arms wide in exasperation. "And pray tell, you silly girl, why would I want to do something like that? I'm the big, bad Beastie, remember? And you're powerless against me."

The Beastie pointed to his chest, voice dripping with hatred. "I'm *born* to cause pain and misery, not let happy families go home so they can sit around and giggle themselves silly, telling stupid stories!"

Mary fixed him with her own dark eyes, unflinching.

"You weren't *born* that way, silly."

"WHAAAT! What is this crazy little girl saying?" He pointed at Mam. "Did she inherit this madness from you, mammy?!"

"There's only one psycho in this room, and he looks like a mutant pig!" whispered Mam fiercely. Aunt Kay snorted loudly.

The Beastie gave an ugly laugh then and glanced down at Tom, lying in a stupor on the cold floor at his feet. "I'm lord here in this castle of blood. If you speak to me like that again, I'll…"

"You owe me another wish!" Mary shouted suddenly.

"You ran out of your wishes, little girl, wasting them on rats and…"

"No! You said I could have a *bonus* wish for being kind to you. You owe me an extra wish. Remember?"

"I don't owe you anything! Get this into your putrid brain; I am *bad!* I am more than bad! I am the evillest thing ever to walk this earth! I'll eat your cat in front of your very eyes for breakfast and wear its furry tail to keep my neck warm! Why… WHY would you expect me to grant you another wish?"

Mary smiled at him, a genuinely warm smile that placed a sliver of doubt into the Beastie's rotten heart.

"Because you promised, and you always keep your promises, don't you?"

The Beastie's eyes widened in amazement.

"I… I… promised?"

"You gave me your *word*…"

An image flashed in Mary's mind of a boy laughing happily beside his mother, who was looking down at him lovingly, sharing a secret joke.

The Beastie lurched back violently at Mary's words

and held his head, eyes shut in sudden agony. At once, Mary, Mam, and Aunt Kay were released from the spell's hold. Mam gave a shout and ran to lift Tom's limp form, shivering, from the murky floor. She cried tears of relief into Tom's chest, who gave a soft moan of recognition and gripped Mam's hair tightly with his chubby hands, which had turned blue and trembling with cold.

Aunt Kay stumbled forward as her legs started running again and bumped against the Beastie. She found herself looking down at the top of his head, her taser gun already pressed hard against his armpit. She squeezed the ON button, screaming:

"*DIE* YOU GREASY MONSTER!!"

Aunt Kay's face went purple with rage, with thick veins protruding from her neck. She was standing right up to him; she could feel his cold flesh through her coat, and the nauseating stink from his bushy hair was sharp in her nose as she screamed, "FEEL THE PAIN OF TWENTY-ONE MILLION VOLTS, PORKYYYYY!!!!" The Beastie's left armpit flashed brightly from the taser gun like a light bulb had just been turned on next to his greasy skin.

The Beastie's body writhed in anticipation of the excruciating agony, his eyes tight shut, while Aunt Kay's hand was right inside his hairy, greasy armpit.

They both then stared into each other's eyes, only a couple of inches away, subsequently looking down at the taser, from where a female computer-generated voice sounded: *flashlight mode in operation.*

Aunt Kay reacted instantaneously, pushing the Beastie away from her, wiping the wet taser gun and her hand on her coat, her face contorted in disgust.

"Well, that was… interesting," said the Beastie, surprised himself, smelling his armpit to make sure it was alright.

"*Ugh…*" Aunt Kay looked faint.

They now faced each other. Mary, Mam carrying Tom, and Aunt Kay on one side, the Beastie with his back to the boiling pot on the other.

"I wish…" began Mary.

"Shut up! There are no more wishes!" cried the Beastie.

"He's just going to twist your words around, honey; turn it into something bad like the other wishes," said Mam.

"Listen to mammy, little Mary," sneered Beastie. "Before something really *bad* happens. Haven't you done enough, giving away your baby brother like that?" The Beastie laughed gleefully as he knew the torment he was causing Mary.

"Here, why don't I take you on a tour of my home instead? I'll show you my favorite toy. I call it the *Grinder*. It's what I use to make flour. And here, care for a scarf?" He went to the pile Tom was lying on earlier, which had initially looked like a pile of furry scarves. He picked one and placed it around Aunt Kay's neck. It was black with a white tip. A strong odor came from one bloody end. Only then did Aunt Kay realize…

"*Aagh!* It's a cat's tail! It's a bloody cat's tail!" screamed Aunt Kay, throwing away the gruesome appendage from around her neck, which left droplets of blood on her coat.

Mary heard Aunt Kay retching violently but kept her gaze locked steadily on her adversary. Tears of sorrow moistened her eyes for all the loved pets that had suffered at the hands of this monster.

Through the grief, she whispered, "I wish for you to leave us alone."

The Beastie fumed at her words, then said in a low growl, "Silly girl. As you wish, little Mary."

CHAPTER 16
A DEADLY GLINT

Obeying Mary's wish, the Beastie turned his back on them and sauntered away, stomping past the boiling pot towards a shadowed corner of the large hall.

Aunt Kay, looking very pale, turned towards the door through which they had entered. "Let's free all these kids and leave this hell hole."

The only thing was, there was no longer a door. Just a solid grey wall, with no sign whatsoever, an entrance had ever existed. Aunt Kay ran and pushed desperately, trying to find some give, a hidden catch, or a faint line to indicate a doorway behind the hard rock.

"Nooo! That murdering scumbag! He cheated us again! Hey, you, get back here!"

They heard a faint chortle echoing from the far corner. "I can't go near you wonderful lot, remember? Just keeping my promise!"

"You're really something else, you know that!" cried Aunt Kay in his direction. "Your *mama* would be really proud of you! What, with all the kidnapping and killing, playing these silly little *games*!"

The Beastie emerged from his corner, trudging slowly towards them in his big, squeaky boots. He stopped just beside the bubbling pot, staring at them quietly, his visage half concealed by steam and shadow. Somehow, the hush seemed more threatening, sending shivers down Mary's spine. The silence stretched for so long that Aunt Kay could not stand it anymore. "What?! Say something, then! Cat got your dirty tongue?"

"No, blondie, the cat could not get anything now, as you had just seen." The Beastie replied in a quiet voice, making Aunt Kay blanch in horror. "As for silly, little games, why yes, I think it's time we play a little game now."

"Look," Mam said firmly, Tom asleep in her arms. "Enough is enough! We just want to go home. You've just witnessed that we can beat you and make life very unpleasant for you down here. Let *us* be on our way, *you* get the hell out of our town, and we'll leave it at that."

Mary knew instinctively Mam was only trying to negotiate something with the Beastie for their sake. If the Beastie agreed and left the city, he would only wreak havoc and misery in other parts of Ireland. For the moment, though, it was one step at a time.

"*And* you went back on your word. You broke my wish to leave us alone," said Mary. The Beastie looked at her with hate-filled eyes.

"Fine then. Let us play a final game now, a game to end this little drama of ours, shall we? If you win, I promise to let you out so you may continue your feeble existence. But if I win, I'm gonna have your marinated livers for breakfast!" The Beastie whooped and clicked his heels in the air, waving about the blade in his hand.

"No deal!" shouted Mam, the noise agitating Tom.

"You're crazy!" fired Aunt Kay.

"I'm *not* giving you a choice!" shrieked the Beastie. He snapped his fingers, and immediately, Mary felt a wave of dread course through her body. She glanced up at Mam and Aunt Kay, who rocked back on their heels, experiencing a similar sensation. But this time, they were still able to move and react.

The Beastie glared at them in astonishment. He clicked his fingers again and again, but the waves of dark energy did not immobilize them as previously. Whatever happened to the Beastie, when Mary began seeing glimpses behind the dark veil of his mind, had counteracted his powers, made his spells less potent.

He was still very dangerous, though, wielding his wickedly sharp blade and holding them ransom with all the other captives. Tom was getting weaker by the minute, too. They needed to get out of there fast.

"What's the game, then?" asked Mary.

"No, Mary!" cried Mam. "He won't keep his word. He'll just manipulate his way out again!"

Mary looked at her mother and the still form of her baby brother. "We have no choice, Mam. Tom's running out of time." The Beastie began to shuffle forward closer towards them, rubbing his hands in glee.

"Such a brave girl you are, little Mary," said the Beastie in delight. "I know just the game for a bright lass like you. Riddles, of course! Ho Ho! We can finally have some fun! Three riddles each. Who will get the most right answers? It's Light versus Dark. Beauties against the Beast!" He finished with a wide smile, displaying his rotten front teeth.

"I kind of prefer it when he was quietly brooding in his corner. Now he's all mouth again," murmured Aunt Kay.

A deadly glint lit up the Beastie's eyes as he looked at her. "We will start with you then, blondie. If you get this first riddle wrong, I'll bite your pretty face off."

CHAPTER 17
WAR OF WORDS

"Just *hold on* there, Hog Breath! Don't you know it's always ladies first? Where are your manners?"

A shadow flitted across the Beastie's face at Aunt Kay's words. He chose to remain silent, seemingly assenting to her request.

"Hah! Not such a tough guy, is he?"

"Don't ever question my manners again, blondie," his voice menacingly low. "It really doesn't matter. It's still three turns each. Go right ahead then, say your riddle…"

Aunt Kay started to sweat, brow furrowed in sudden panic.

"What? You mean right now?!… Ok, a riddle… huh… can't be that tough. Think, Kay, think! What was that movie again, small ugly fellow obsessed with a ring? Sorta looks like a slimmed-down version of Pork Chops here?"

Mary started to whisper something to Aunt Kay as the Beastie glowered over them.

"This is good, Mary. Can you repeat that? Ger, what about you? Any ideas? I wouldn't look too good without a nose!" Both Mam and Mary whispered more suggestions to Aunt Kay.

"Hey, you're cheating!" cried the Beastie.

"Cheating my butt! It's Beauties against the Beast, remember? So, it's all of us against you!"

The Beastie gnashed his teeth at them. "It wouldn't make any difference anyway. I am a Master Riddler! I have lived through centuries, studied the human mind…"

"Ok, got one!" declared Aunt Kay. "*Good thinking, Mary,*" she winked. "*Ehmm…* right, here goes…"

"Similar in name, same in height
"Like pretty twin sisters having a fight
"By putting us down, we raise you up
"Perfect match for fur and makeup!"

"Say that again?" said the Beastie.

"Hah! Woo hoo, we got him! He's stumped! He'll never get this one! Who's the brainy one in this family, huh??! Woo hoo!" shouted Aunt Kay, flinging her arms up high, so happy that she did a hop, skip and jump, drawing the Beastie's attention down to her…

"Boots...! No... shoes? No... high heels? Yesss!!! The answer is a pair of *high heels!* Ho ho! Nice little dance there, blondie."

Aunt Kay froze midstride like she was hit by another spell bolt, suddenly deflated. She gave an apologetic shake of the head to the others. Mary gave her a smile of reassurance. "No worries, Aunt Kay, it's not over yet."

"Now, it's my turn." The Beastie puffed up his hairy chest and bellowed:

"A grumble, a growl
"Foul wind to boot
"I gnash, I maul
"All that was chewed!"

"He's not being too generous with his words, is he?" said Mam. "What the heck is it? A dog growling or something?"

"But what's the wind about?" asked Aunt Kay.

"Maybe he's talking about an eagle?" said Mam.

The Beastie smiled slyly at their confusion, rubbing his hands on his furry chest in delight. Just then, a large rat ran behind his legs, clutching a piece of rotten meat in its jaws. In a flash, the Beastie stabbed down with his claws, piercing the squealing rat with one sharp talon. In one fluid motion, he chomped down on the rat's upper body, making revolting crunching sounds, before swallowing the rest of the poor animal, smacking his lips as the rat's tail disappeared into his mouth. He tapped his stomach in satisfaction and belched loudly, permeating the air with a revolting semi-digested rat scent.

"What makes a grumbling sound when empty, then gives off foul air when full? Why, it's the *stomach*. The answer is stomach!" cried Mary, triumphantly. The Beastie roared in disgust.

"Ha Ha! Score one for the Beauties! Stomach? Is that all you think about, your stomach?! Hah!" clapped Aunt Kay. Mam smiled at Mary.

"I guess it's my turn now," Mam said.

Mary tapped her arm, and as her Mam crouched close to her, Mary whispered another idea for a riddle behind her cupped hand.

"YOU'RE CHEATING!" screamed the Beastie, spittle flecking his beard.

"Keep your pants on! I'm ready!" shouted back Mam.

"Yeah! Please do keep your pants on, Hairy Butts!" shouted Aunt Kay.

Mam stepped forward, cracking her neck like a fighter, and said:

"Once *a day, thrice a week*

"Go away sorrow, farewell reek
"My name's a place, on many a map
"Full to bursting, right turn tap!"

"Come on then, Mr Beastie! Give us your best shot!" Mam punched her fist in the air.

The Beastie's face swelled up in fierce concentration. He started hopping on his boots, his bushy hair standing on end.

"We're waiting!" hollered Aunt Kay.

The Beastie howled in rage, went down on all fours, and started running around them in circles, grunting in frustration.

Aunt Kay could not keep her excitement down; she did so love to win. She clapped her hands and said to the others, "Ha ha! Old stinky here will never get the answer. I doubt he ever had one!"

"*Shhh!* Aunt Kay," Mary warned as the Beastie's sharp ears caught her words. He started to slow down his rampage as he began to digest the riddle. He stopped right in front of Aunt Kay and stood straight up. He smiled in pleasure as the answer dawned on him.

"Hmmm… it is a good riddle, brilliant even. You're right there, blondie. I would never have guessed. I've never taken a *bath* in all my life."

Aunt Kay looked down at her boots guiltily. Bath

is the answer to their second riddle. Mam sighed heavily in exasperation.

"My turn now, ladies," said the Beastie, strutting confidently again in front of them. He told his next riddle while staring at them greedily, smacking his lips at the thought of roasting their sweet flesh.

"Bones boiling, fat churning
"My, my, what a fine dish!
"Witches cackling, mothers crying
"Why, why, throw away that wish?
"Darkness creeping, children weeping
"Cry, cry, sweet dreams tarnish!"

"What is he on about? First, it's his stomach, now he's actually preparing a dish?" said Aunt Kay, keen to make amends for giving away the first two answers. "Ugh, I can't bear to even guess what he likes to eat. Probably a dead dog or something."

"No, he's just mixing up his words. It's not food. It's something else. Maybe it's to do with the wishes Mary made, you know, back at the flat," said Mam.

"That's it!" cried Aunt Kay. "The flour! Remember, he said he made the flour using that grinding machine? So, maybe that's the dish he's preparing." Aunt Kay turned to Mary. "What do you think, honey? It has to be the flour, right?"

Mary kept silent. She looked at the Beastie, who was visibly salivating at this stage. He must have overheard them talking with his sharp, pointy ears and knew they were on the wrong track.

"We have the answer, Beastie!" announced Aunt Kay. At that moment, Tom began to whimper in his sleep. Mary could see his eyes moving rapidly behind his eyelids, his tiny hands outstretched, like he was warding off something in his sleep.

Mary recalled the words of the riddle.

...*Darkness creeping, children weeping*
Cry, cry, sweet dreams tarnish...

"Prepare to admit defeat, you creep!" shouted Aunt Kay. "The answer is your stinking flo..."

"Wait! Stop, that's not it!" cried Mary.

"Let her finish the answer, you silly girl!" screeched the Beastie, veins popping from his neck.

"It's *nightmare*. The answer to your final riddle is nightmare," said Mary.

The Beastie once again roared in anger and frustration, his eyes staining red from burst veins. He clenched his fists so tightly that his sharp nails dug deeply into his palms.

"Three to us, two to Mr. Pork Pie, ha ha! We'll be home soon!" shouted Aunt Kay.

Mam and Aunt Kay then each looked at Mary, who nodded to them in understanding. "I have to say the final riddle."

"Of course, it has to be you, you *Terrible Sister!* Giving away your baby brother like that. All this is your fault!" taunted the Beastie.

"Don't listen to him, Mary," said Mam. "You can do it, girl! We believe in you."

"Yeah, Luv. Forget hairy Humpty Dumpty over there!" said Aunt Kay.

Mary took a deep breath to compose herself. She must not fail this time. She must be brave. She looked at Mam, Aunt Kay, and Tom, who were all depending on her, before saying her riddle.

> *"The first of many, so listen intently*
> *"Middle of a woman is one too many*
> *"Love, hugs, soup and spaghetti*
> *"That's the end of my sore tummy!"*

"That makes absolutely no sense at all," cried Beastie. "What a terrible riddle. You're cheating again! Doesn't even rhyme well!"

Aunt Kay gave Mary a thumbs up and nudged Mam. "I haven't a clue what the girl just said, but it sounded brilliant!"

To the Beastie, she mocked, "For someone who's

never had a bath, you're very picky with your riddles."

The Beastie twiddled his thumbs nervously, turning his back on them. He murmured out loud the possible answers to himself, "What's the middle of a woman? Her stomach! Not one but two? A woman doesn't have two stomachs. Maybe she's a cow? Cows have four stomachs. Wait, how did I know that? Who cares! Yes, that's got to be it! *A cow and ...and... which has a sore tummy from eating grass that looks like spaghetti!!* Yes! I'm a genius!!"

The Beastie turned back to face Mary, a triumphant grin on his face. "The answer is a cow with a sore tummy from eating grass that looks..." His voice trailed off, and he stopped himself with a frown as Mary shook her head. "This is not a fair game. Say the riddle to me again. Perhaps it's the way you *say* it that's confusing me."

"Hey, no way!" said Aunt Kay defiantly. "*You're* the one who wanted this game, *Master* Riddler. C'mon then, give us the answer. Or do you give up?"

"Never!" cried the Beastie.

"It's ok, Aunt Kay. I'll repeat the riddle again."

"But..."

Mary looked up at her aunt, a strange light in her eyes. "Trust me..."

"Sure, honey. I trust you. Go for it."

Mary repeated her words:

"The first of many, so listen intently
"Middle of a woman is one too many
"Love, hugs, soup and spaghetti
"That's the end of my sore tummy!"

"Ha ha! The thrill of victory is sweet indeed," jeered Aunt Kay at the Beastie, who was pulling his hair out and gnashing his teeth in despair. He had absolutely no idea what Mary was hinting at in her riddle.

"We're going home! Home, sweet home! Here, let me take Tom from you, Ger; you must be knackered."

"No, I'm fine, Kay. I don't want him to wake up," said Mam, gently swaying a sleeping Tom in her arms.

"No, I insist! I'll hold him while you rest." Aunt Kay lifted Tom from Mam's arms.

But this caused Tom to wake up in a fright, his eyes wide open, crying, "Mammy," his very first word!

The Beastie pricked up his ears as Mary looked at her brother in sudden fear. For the Beastie, although very crude in many ways, was certainly nobody's fool. He had not lived to be centuries old without a cunning brain and an opportunistic nature. His frustrated demeanor slowly lifted as he mulled over the events unfolding in front of his very eyes.

"The first of many... hmmm... could that mean a baby? No, it's not that obvious. Could the brat mean the first *letters* of the word many? Which would be M and A. *Ahh...* I see where we're going here. Next, the middle of the word woman is the letter M. One too many... so maybe two MMs! And the end of the word tummy is Y. Join them together, and we get the word MAMMY... Ho Ho, very clever little Mary, very clever indeed."

Aunt Kay gave Tom back to Mam.

"Yes, Beastie, the answer is Mammy, Mother, Mama... or Mam. Do these words mean anything to you?" said Mary gently.

"What do you mean, you silly little girl?" retorted back the Beastie, his black heart quickening in sudden panic.

Mary walked right up to him, causing the Beastie to retreat a few steps, surprise and confusion in his eyes. Without any hesitation, Mary placed her hands on the sides of the Beastie's head, staring right into his eyes, searching for something or someone...

The Beastie started to tremble. Never in all the centuries had someone held him like this before. He stammered out his next words, "Get your hands off me, what do you think..."

"It's your turn now."

"WHAT are you talking about!?" The Beastie stood transfixed, quivering in Mary's hold.

"It's your turn. Your last riddle. Speak it now!" Mary commanded, her voice amplified, echoing in the vast hall.

At Mary's order, the Beastie's eyes lighted up strangely. His trembling subsided, and a calm fell across his features. Mary stepped back and gave him an encouraging smile.

"Go on then, let's hear it," she urged softly.

When next the Beastie spoke, it was not the hoarse voice of an old man nor the growl of a monster that they heard, but what came out from his lips was the voice of a boy, a very young boy.

"I live, I breathe
"I rage, I cleave
"I knock, I grin
"I devour hearts within
"I know, wholly darkness
"My road, only blindness
"No joy, no relief
"Utter despair, under every leaf
"One such as you, I have never met
"So tell me why I burn with hatred?
"Why was I born as a monster?
"Was I ever, even a toddler?
"Every child, sired by some father

"Which woman had I called mother?
"For who would want a thing like me
"Not a one, not even out of pity
"For as surely as day follows night
"A horned baby is killed at first sight
"Thus, I ask you again, o' wise little girl
"Was I always so wicked, so utterly cruel?
"With this beastly face and voice so rough
"Whom not even a mother would ever love?"

Mary, Mam, and Aunt Kay stood in utter shock, absolutely flabbergasted to hear the Beastie speak so eloquently. His expression was one of profound longing and sadness, with bloody tears running down his cheeks. But it was his voice, that of a child's, that broke their hearts.

Mary stepped close to the Beastie again, her moist brown eyes level with his green, so close he could have reached out and torn off her face if he had wanted to. Instead, he kept still as Mary held up her clenched fist right in front of his face.

"The answer that you've been searching for is in here."

Mary opened her fingers, revealing a small glass vial containing a dark, golden liquid. She removed the stopper and, before anyone could react, flung the contents straight at the Beastie's face. The liquid flew in a sparkling wave of gold as the intoxicating aromas of jasmine and lavender burst forth and filled the air.

The perfumed oil splashed into his lifeless eyes, surged up his nose, and flew into his open mouth straight down his throat.

The Beastie screamed in silent agony, raking deep grooves into his neck with his sharp nails. He heard the blast of a thousand thunderbolts as an iron wall shattered in his mind.

The Beastie looked at Mary for what seemed an eternity before his eyes rolled up in their sockets, and he fell forwards into the murk, splashing Mary with bloody goo, and lay unconscious as darkness finally seized him.

CHAPTER 18
A MILLION JAGGED PIECES

A young, scrawny boy was running swiftly, fear driving his haggard body onwards. A full blood moon cast a baleful red glow over the ancient swamps of Kildare, causing a bewildering assortment of shadows to crisscross the narrow path meandering through the misty marshland.

Deep, treacherous bog water lay just inches away from his bare feet as he splashed along the soggy path. His breath came in ragged wheezes as he looked back, desperation lending his thin legs some semblance of strength though he had been starved for days.

He could hear them now, the ravenous baying of wolfhounds, their mistresses close behind, whooping and howling in their bloodlust. They were gaining on him, and he was getting weaker.

The boy had escaped his captors, having spent many

terrible days and nights locked in a cage in anticipation of his sacrifice. The witches had fed him nothing, with only rainwater gathered in a bowl to sustain him.

His empty stomach grumbling painfully, he was forced to scavenge for bugs and beetles amongst the filth of his prison. Flashes of his mother's face had come to him often, comforting him throughout his dark, lonely ordeal, ever since that frightful night when they had dragged him away from his home, where he had been happy, warm, and safe.

His mother had cooked his favorite hotchpotch stew that fateful evening for dinner, with plenty of extra cuts of tender mutton and vegetables swimming in his bowl. He finished the last of his meal, lifting the bowl so the last of the gravy poured deliciously down his throat.

"Thank you, Mam. That was the best stew I ever tasted."

"Would you like seconds, Tadgh?" she had asked with a smile, knowing full well his answer. "Yes, please, Mam. Thank you." Tadgh answered.

His mother had always taught him good manners. "Manners are what makes a man, son, not riches or land. And always keep your promises! A man's word is his honor".

"I will Mam, I promise."

His mother had hugged him and tucked him into bed. She would always tell him funny bedtime tales and silly stories. That night, she told his favorite, the story of a hungry cow with four stomachs and a lucky lizard who grew a new tail. He had laughed so hard he cried happy tears. They chatted for a long time like that, him lying in his bed of straw, his mam sitting next to him, holding his hand. Then, to his delight, she hummed his favorite lullaby until he fell asleep, curled up in his usual way, dreaming sweet dreams.

Then, at midnight, his little world shattered into a million jagged pieces.

Thirteen black cowled figures surrounded their isolated little hut. Long, dank, greasy hair covered faces twisted with malice, claw-like nails protruding from bony hands. They muttered spells of silence and concealment, desperate as they were to claim their prize.

The Celtic coven of witches had existed for centuries on the island, their dark origins shrouded in mystery. As one member perishes, a new initiate would be chosen to take her place, always to maintain the thirteen strong. Tonight, they desired to obtain the main ingredient for their annual sacrifice as part of a black ritual of the Celtic witches stretching back eons. Through their animal familiars, they had located this isolated hut that housed a child suitable for their vile purpose. They approached it now, the pale moonlight casting their crooked shadows across the damp earth and mudbrick wall.

With a touch of a twisted oak staff, the simple wooden door shattered inwards. As already premeditated, eight of the witches immediately approached the larger prone figure of Tadgh's mother, illuminated by the dying fire in the hearth.

Cold, hard fingers covered Tadgh's mouth and eyes, his befuddled mind still groggy from sleep and the shock of the door exploding. He barely managed a weak cry when they bundled his small body roughly into a damp, hessian sack. He was carried, then dragged, along a hard, bumpy road for the longest time. The dirt road then felt wet and slippery under his body. He whimpered and sobbed fearfully in the darkness of the sack, crying out for his mother, but only received a hard kick from an iron-toed boot, silencing him.

The witches trudged on with astonishing speed, the hags and their animal companions covering a great distance on foot. He could hear their cruel cackles and screams of delight, punctuated by barks and caws.

Tadgh began to feel hard stones beneath him, their sharp edges digging painfully into his sides. Finally, after an eternity of bumps, lumps, and suffocating darkness, they stopped. The sack was untied, and Tadgh was bundled inside a cage of meshed branches of birch, too cramped to allow him to stand or stretch his legs. He stared in terror at the thirteen pairs of benevolent eyes gazing down at him. The hags encircled his tiny cage, thirteen women in black, filthy smocks, hoods drawn back to reveal their cruel faces under lank, greasy hair.

They pierced and scratched him with their long fingernails through the boughs of his wooden prison, laughing and jeering, black lips twisting into grotesque smiles. Even through his terror, he gagged from the foul stench of their unwashed bodies and mouths, assailing his already shocked senses.

After long moments of playing with him, the witches grew bored and left him alone while they lounged on the stony floor. One particularly vile creature who tormented him to no end called herself Glitter, leader of this coven of witches.

It was a strange choice for a name, thought young Tadgh, when she had first introduced herself, in a mockery of comradeship. The ugly hag was anything but glittery. Her stringy hair framed a bloated face, dominated by a hairy, warty chin that jutted over her cracked lips in an overbite. She would come up to his cage when he was asleep and poke him in the face with her filthy claw. She would taunt him with threats of what was to come and kept him awake with riddles, shaking his cage like a crazed baboon if he did not respond.

Pushing her ugly face through his cage, Glitter would sing in a revolting, croaky voice, spraying spittle in his face:

"Roses are red
"Violets are blue
"Little boys bled
"When chopped in two!"

Another of the horrid hag's favorites was:

"Who? Coughs and sneezes
"Where? Blows the breezes
"Why? Mice love cheeses
"What? Chokes with wheezes
"When? I grab and squeezes!"

Or other similar horrendous rhymes and riddles that her mad mind kept conjuring up. Tadgh would huddle away fearfully, making Glitter scream more insults at him. Even worse than the nightly taunts was the dreadful reek from her large body, causing him to retch whenever she came close.

Glitter delighted in describing in vivid detail his looming sacrifice in the night of the blood moon, then just a few nights away. He trembled with fear at the thought, causing the foul hag to point and shout at him. "It's only a snip and a snap, boy! There's nothing to be scared about. You should be looking forward to it. Why, you're the guest of honor, waited hand and foot by thirteen beautiful ladies!" With that, the whole cavern shook with their coarse laughter.

***

From what Tadgh could make out, they were located deep inside a large cavern, long stalactites pointing like daggers from the rocky ceiling, the constant sound of dripping water echoing off the stone walls.

The only light source was from a green, smoky fire kept perpetually lit under a bubbling black cauldron, into which the witches kept dropping pungent herbs, bugs, rats, and other small creatures. These they would fish out whenever they were hungry, using a long wooden ladle, and slurped noisily in front of him. He would sometimes hear the rough barks and growls of large dogs coming from somewhere in the unseen distance.

One of these hounds went sniffing close to his cage. It resembled a feral wolf with long black fur and a sharp snout, its inch-long fangs visible in the half-light. It stared at him with hungry eyes, saliva dripping from its maw, until a sharp kick from one of the witches sent it whining on its way.

Tadgh did not know what had happened to his mother, and he was too afraid to ask any of the witches, fearing the worst. *Is Mam still alive, and is she worried that I'm gone so long?* he thought in deep sorrow. Mice and voles kept him company, scurrying over his legs and arms whenever he lay to sleep.

One time, a small group of five witches left the cave and returned a few hours later, hefting in the carcass of a giant boar over their shoulders hanging from a long branch, accompanied by the yelping hounds, suggesting these witches would also venture out to hunt. They dumped the boar close to his cage, red eyes staring unblinkingly from its tusked head.

Two of the witches, one skinny as a stick with wild wiry hair and the other stout with a mean face, began butchering the carcass, hacking it with their rusty iron knives, all the while eyeing him with cruel amusement. Blood and vile black liquid seeped from the carcass into his cage, forcing him to push dirt with his feet to block the flow from reaching him. The worst part was when they cooked the meat on sharp sticks over the fire, the smell causing Tadgh to feel faint with hunger.

Apart from the wolfhounds, Tadgh studied the other animal familiars which roamed about the cave. Each witch seemed to favor one particular animal, consisting of crows, large black rats, and toads. He was not aware of the concept of witch familiars, but he surmised there was a special bond between a witch and a particular animal, feeding and talking to it like a pet. These familiars also appeared larger and meaner than their ordinary animal counterparts.

He hated the toads and rats the most. They would creep up to his cage when he was asleep, then slither in between the boughs, jumping and scampering over his face and hands, dashing away out of reach whenever he tried catching them.

One particular familiar, a solitary raven, perched on a large branch on the other side of the cauldron from where Tadgh was imprisoned. The large predatory bird, twice as large as the crows, was usually blocked from his view by the smoke. What was clear was that the bird was Glitter's favorite pet, which she frequently kept feeding with small vermin.

But there was one moment of terror for Tadgh as the raven seemed to sense him looking at it. It glared back with its black beady eyes and screamed, in a disturbingly humanlike voice, *"Tadghhhh!!!! Tadghhhh!!!!"*

An icy shiver ran down Tadgh's spine, and he avoided looking in its direction from then on.

CHAPTER 19
GLIMMER OF HOPE

Tadhg lost track of time in that gloomy cavern. He fretted constantly for his mother while his joints and muscles ached from sitting for so long in that cramped prison of wood, his mind dulled by prolonged hunger and anxiety.

His cage had been crudely constructed, more a mental boundary than a real prison. The witches were confident the small boy's fear would keep him docile. Tadgh kept having recurring nightmares of him being tied hand and foot at the center of a large stone slab, Glitter brandishing a rusty iron blade high above his chest, only to wake up screaming as the blade plummeted towards his exposed skin.

Time passed inexorably towards the appointed night for the coven to enact their bloody ritual. As the hour of the sacrifice drew close, the vile hags worked themselves up into a crazed frenzy, swallowing a bitter-smelling drink they had concocted in the cauldron. Some screamed over and over a name that sent shivers down the boy's spine, clawed hands raised towards the green fire in worship, while others rolled in the dirt, frothing in the mouth, only the whites of their eyes visible in their sockets.

The wolfhound familiars shared the excitement, biting each other before hunting for mice and voles in the dark corners and ripping them apart. Some of these poor critters ran into his cage in desperation to escape the larger predators. It was one such mouse that led to his escape.

For some days, he had been observing a small grey mouse enter his cell, then go out to run at full pelt towards the nearby wall and seemed to vanish. It was not obvious at first how this happened, but by changing his position slightly to the side, Tadgh was able to see a hole in the wall, large enough to accommodate his thin frame.

A small glimmer of hope kindled in his young heart. So he waited, biding his time and conserving his meager strength. But there was always some hag passing by or watching, and in Glitter's case, gloating and needling him with a sharp stick.

He had all but given up hope of ever escaping

when, one night, a shriek went up amongst the coven sisters that the hour was upon them, that a moon in the shade of blood had arisen. The effect was instantaneous, the crones jumping and dancing, eager to get the ritual over and done with, the one that would appease their dark master and guarantee them special favors.

It was during this time that the boy took his chance. He squeezed his bony shoulders through a gap in the wooden boles onto the compact earth, which was littered with the bones of small birds and rabbits, the smoke from the fire further concealing his escape.

Thus, while all eyes were away from him, Tadgh gathered up his courage and crawled towards the hole in the wall. He expected any moment to be stepped on by an iron-shod boot or pierced through his back by a long, sharp stick. He crawled faster and faster, not daring to look back, hoping, praying the hole was big enough that it would take him far away from this horrid place and take him back to his mother.

As Tadgh reached the wall, he saw the same mouse looking at him from the entrance to the hole as if waiting for him, willing him on. The mouse turned and disappeared inside. This spurred the scared little boy on. He crawled into the inky blackness of the low tunnel, its walls scrapping and chaffing his shoulders. His palms and knees crunched on small pebbles and bits of bone.

Onwards, he crawled, ignoring the stifling air and his rising panic that the roof would collapse and choke him in its stony grip. Sweat and dirt stung his eyes, pain burning in his hands and knees from a dozen cuts. Sudden cries of rage and murderous fury from behind warned him that his escape had been discovered. Worse still came the sharp barks and growls of their large dogs, predators that would easily pick up his scent and follow his hidden trail.

At long last, Tadgh clambered out the tunnel exit, the night breeze cooling his wounds, the full moon casting everything in an unearthly red glow. He had no idea where he was, having spent the entirety of his young life beside his mother in their thatched hut and small garden.

Tadgh now ran for his life, tears of fear and loneliness streaming down his face. The sound of fluttering wings came from above him, and Tadgh knew it was Glitter's pet, also joining in the hunt. His vision blurred from exhaustion, the strength all but gone from his legs. He risked one glance behind him. The foremost wolfhound, a fearsome grey shaggy beast, was so close now that he could feel its hot breath on his back. Yet he would keep running. He yelled for his mother in desperation.

The small boy slipped and fell headlong into the deep bog, the freezing, dirty water covering his eyes and mouth. His last thought was of his mother and how lonely she would be without him…

***

Tadgh was floating, standing still in the bog water, arms outstretched in front of him, the moonlight casting his surroundings in dark red. His chest was not moving, full as it was with the black water, the ground far away in the inky darkness.

He felt his heart first fluttering very fast, so fast his brain struggled to keep count. Then he noticed the *dib-dab, dib-dab* of his heart weakening and slowing down until he could count them in his darkening mind… 20, 15, 10 beats.

His eyes closed shut as he again thought with sorrow about his mother and not being able to say his goodbyes. At least he got away from the witches and their awful pets. He consoled himself that they could not proceed with their black sacrifice without him.

CHAPTER 20
FOR MY MAM

Sadly, that was not the end for young Tadgh.

Without the boy to offer in sacrifice, the witch clan was deprived of their bloody ritual. They screeched their outrage, pulling at their greasy hair and scratching their necks and faces in frustration.

Then Glitter, the cruelest and most vile amongst them, declared that all was not lost, that their dark intentions could still be salvaged. With an evil glim in her eyes, Glitter proposed a variation of the ritual, one that had never been attempted in centuries. It was a deed so foul that even the hardiest of the group voiced their reluctance. But such was Glitter's zeal and influence that the others gave their acquiescence.

Hence, with dawn threatening to end this long, dark night, they conducted the ritual. They threw into the same bog the carcasses of a pregnant sow and goat, stolen from the nearest farm. They chanted their ancient spells, holding hands at the black water's edge, their hounds whining fearfully at their feet.

As the first bubbles appeared on the surface, the youngest of the clan screamed in fear and ran back to their cave. One after the other, the witches hurried back, suddenly losing heart, afraid of what they had conjured.

Even Glitter, the last to leave, did not stay long enough to see what would emerge from the depths of the bog where the small, scrawny boy had gone under.

***

Tadgh made his way back to his hut, his fleeting memories telling him this was where he was happy, where he was warm once. He knocked on the door like he had always done, just like his mother had taught him.

Knock...

Knock...

Knock...

There was no answer. He kept knocking for a long time. Finally, he pushed the door open and saw what the witches had done to his poor Mam.

Tadhg walked up to his mother's side and placed her cold hands against his cheeks, just like she had used to do. For the longest time, he stayed like this before kissing her blessed forehead in farewell. No tears fell from his eyes, for he was now beyond sadness, beyond sorrow.

Tadgh was also beyond fear. He was no longer afraid. He walked all the way back to the cave, where he found the thirteen witches sitting in silence around their green fire.

When they saw him, they fell back in fear and disgust, shouting for him to leave them alone. Their hounds cowered in terror, sensing a predator far deadlier than them, the raven squawking in panic near the cave roof.

But Tadgh was devoid of any human sentiment except his need for vengeance. Vengeance he felt fiercely in his little heart, consuming his very being. He stared through lifeless, yellow eyes at each hag's wrinkled face, stopping at Glitter's hideous visage. They picked up their sharp sticks and rocks, brandishing them in his face, spitting their magic-laced curses.

Tadgh roared his hatred, the bloodlust boiling to a crescendo inside his gut, spreading like wildfire throughout his body. With his maw wide open, revealing blackened fangs, he barrelled headlong into their midst, punching, kicking, biting, and slashing with beast-like ferocity. Several of the hags, bloodied and broken, tried to run away, but he chased them down, dragging them by their filthy boots back into the cave. With his bare hands, enhanced by the strength of the animals the witches themselves had endowed him with through their twisted magics, he crushed the life out of each one of them.

Tadhg left Glitter till last. She cried piteously for mercy that she would be his obedient slave and carry out his every whim. *"This is for my Mam,"* he whispered into her ear before plunging his canines into her neck.

Not one of the witches escaped his fury. He counted thirteen to be sure. He then rummaged amongst the ashes around the fire until he found a long, sharp iron rod before turning his attention to the wolfhounds. They howled in fear as he approached, his spear promising a painful end.

But a memory of a dream, a flash of his mother's face, stayed his hand.

"Will you have seconds, Tadgh?" His mam teased with a smile, knowing full well his answer. *They were back at home, in their comfortable little hut that Tadgh knew so well, the peat fire giving a soft, warm glow. The pleasant aroma of lamb stew filled his nostrils.*

"Yes, please, Mam. Thank you."

"You're welcome, son."

Then, his mother's face turned sad as she continued to look at him.

"What's wrong, Mam? Are you feeling alright?"

"I want you to listen to me, son. I have something very important to say to you. You have always been a good boy, and I know you will do what I tell you to."

"Of course, Mam, what is it? Why are you talking like this?"

"We don't have much time together."

A solitary tear ran down his mother's cheek as she cupped his face with her warm hand.

"I am going away, son. You have been the best boy any mother could have, and I'm very proud of you."

"Wait! Where are you going?" Tadgh cried in alarm, reaching for his mother as his vision began to blur and his mother's voice grew faint.

"Remember everything I've taught you, son. I will always love you."

Tadgh now stood still and watched silently as the hounds scampered out of the cave. Of the raven and other familiars, there was not a trace.

As the dawn sun lightened the sky, the creature, who was once a boy, crawled into the tunnel at the back of the cave. He curled up on the ground, the way he used to sleep in his bed, listening to his Mam's lullaby. A small grey mouse kept him company, snuggling inside his paws. He fell into a long, deep slumber.

Only when the temperature plummeted, as the

first snow of the great frost appeared, did he begin to stir and open his eyes. He found white bone dust in his hairy hands, with all remnants of his memories vanished, hidden behind a rigid wall of iron.

CHAPTER 21
BODY OF A MONSTER

Memories hidden until now.

The Beastie felt a small hand on his own.

"I'm so sorry," whispered Mary, tears flowing freely down her face. "I'm sorry you lost your Mam, for what they did to you."

The sweet fragrances of lavender and jasmine permeated the stifling air of the hall, the only sounds emanating from the bubbling pot.

"My Mam..." the Beastie said quietly. He stared at Mary, then at Mam and Aunt Kay. He looked down at his hands, which he brought up to touch his face. He walked slowly to the pot. He clambered up the stool and looked at the churning surface.

With one word, the bubbles ceased, leaving a clear surface of liquid. He looked at his reflection long and hard as if seeing himself for the first time before the harsh bubbling and hissing resumed, the gruel boiling away at the bottom.

The Beastie stepped down from the stool and faced them. "I… I… remember," he said, trembling with the unspeakable burden of discovered memories and emotions.

"What's wrong with the fella?" asked Aunt Kay. "What's he remembering?"

"Everything," answered Mary softly. It was unbearable for Mary to see his torment. She had seen through the iron wall in his mind, which was like a metal glove clutching his brain in its grip. She had not seen full visions, more snatches of emotions and impressions, brief sparks of voices, faces, and smells. But these had been enough for her sharp mind to piece together the unfathomable horrors the Beastie had experienced to make him what he was now, what the young boy, Tadgh, no older than she was, had been put through. A young boy trapped in the body of a monster.

A stillness befell the group. With the soft light of the chandelier, Mary noticed three shadows extending from the Beastie, each one different from the other: a shadow of a large hairy pig extended from his right, that of a bearded, horned goat from his left, and that of a thin boy extended from his front towards them.

Suddenly, these three shadows speared to retract, becoming shorter and gathering at his feet. The Beastie, too, seemed stunned as he watched his own shadow travel up his legs, his body, and finally to the top of his head. From here, it coalesced into the shape of a large black bird and, with a flap of its shadowy wings, launched up to the high ceiling and disappeared.

Everyone was looking up, searching the ceiling, when they heard a rasping cackle floating from a far corner of the roof. They all peered into the gloom. It came again, a grating giggle of pure malice that sent shivers of ice down Mary's spine. The large black shadow erupted from its hiding place and flew back and forth above them. It landed on the chandelier in a flutter of wings and peered down at them with black beady eyes.

They looked up at the bird as it crawled all over the chandelier like a bat, cackling and giggling in an eerie, harsh female voice. The chandelier swung haphazardly, causing distorted shadows to fleet dizzyingly around the group below. The bird left its perch and dropped like a bullet on outstretched feathery wings towards them. It flew directly for Aunt Kay's head, clawing at her hair, then launching off with strands of her blonde hair in its sharp claws before she could even react. It landed on the floor at the far side of the hall, Aunt Kay gasping in pain as she placed her hand onto her bloodied scalp.

Now that they could see it properly, it had the appearance of a very large crow or a raven. A low growl came from Mary's side. She glanced at the Beastie, who was glaring at the bird predator with wide, hate-filled eyes, his hands clenching and unclenching. He appeared to be on the verge of rushing at the bird when the light from the chandelier suddenly went out, plunging the room into total darkness.

"Oh no, not again. I hate the dark," moaned Aunt Kay. She seemed to be fiddling with something.

Then came a click: *flashlight mode in operation.*

A bright beam of light streamed across the hall towards the spot where the raven was. Only it was not a bird anymore. Instead, an old woman stood facing them, one with a warty chin that protruded out from her blotchy face. Even from this distance, they could smell the reek wafting in nauseating waves from her large body, which was covered in a moldy black dress, under which peeked tips of iron-shod boots.

Worst of all was her hair. As the flashlight fell on her, her hair shimmered and sparkled with a hundred stars, long, fizzy blonde hair, just like Aunt Kay's.

"Glitter," murmured the Beastie through clenched teeth.

"Hello, Tadgh," the hag crooned, flicking her long blonde hair back over one shoulder. "Missed me?"

This time, the Beastie did surge forth, resuming his monster features, black claws extended, his maw wide open in a mindless shriek, his own black boots pumping on the wet ground.

"What the..." said Aunt Kay, flabbergasted, dropping the taser in shock, plunging the hall once more into darkness as the bulb shattered on the ground.

They could hear the noise the Beastie made as he stomped and raved at the far end of the hall, seemingly running around in circles. Then, after several tense minutes, they heard him breathing heavily, punctuated by guttural growls of frustration.

Then, they heard the sharp snap of fingers clicking, and the room brightened once again, the light from the chandelier blazing too brightly after the gloom. The Beastie was no longer there, nor the croon. Mary gazed up and searched the ceiling, but there was no sign of the raven either.

CHAPTER 22
DREAMLESS SLEEP

"Hey, there's something in here," said Aunt Kay.

In the middle of the warehouse floor was a green bowler hat, which no one had not noticed until then.

Aunt Kay walked up to it and noticed several shiny objects inside. She took out a thick band of gold, one of the Beastie's rings. A total of ten solid gold rings were in the hat.

"Wow, do you think he left these for us?" asked Aunt Kay.

"Well, hopefully," Mam said, as Mary hugged Tom tightly and kissed his grimy face. "If he did, we won't have to worry about money to buy flour anymore."

Earlier, as soon as they had gotten over the shock of the recent events, they hurried over to the first of the children's cages. A pale girl, no older than seven, stared out hopefully through the bars of her cage. Her head was covered with patchy tufts of hair, and her ragged, filthy rags hardly concealed her thin frame. She pointed a shaky finger at a metal hook on a nearby wall, from which hung a large brass key.

Aunt Kay immediately fetched the key and, within moments, had unlocked all the cage doors and freed the children. They crawled or limped unsteadily out of their prisons, twenty boys and girls in all.

"The door is still missing," said Mam, indicating the wall through which they had entered earlier. Mary handed Tom to Mam and stared at the wall, tapping her fingers on her chin shrewdly. She then took the key from Aunt Kay and stepped right up to the wall.

"Hope this works," she muttered under her breath and touched the key to where she thought the door was supposed to be. As soon as the key touched the wall, the Beastie's illusion was lifted, and the door reappeared. Everyone cheered as Mary unlocked it, and a cool breeze wafted in, bringing instant relief from the heat and stench.

"Please follow me in a straight line," commanded Mary. The weak children obeyed immediately and began shuffling out of that room of horror with Mam, Tom, and Aunt Kay bringing up the rear. Aunt Kay looked downcast and pale, dried blood caking her forehead and scalp, where the raven had ripped away some of her hair.

Mary's mind was numb as she led the group out. She had just witnessed too much, experienced more than any ten-year-old had the right to in many lifetimes, that she just wanted to curl up somewhere and forget everything, even for just a short while.

They found a short flight of steps, real steps this time as the illusion had vanished, leading down into a warehouse packed with moldy boxes. They avoided a freshly squished dead rat (*"Me bad,"* mumbled Aunt Kay), crossed to the adjacent room, and tumbled out the back door to find the sky starting to take on the pre-dawn hue.

They were a woeful sight for anyone who would happen to see them, covered head to toe in muck and grime as if they had spent the night in the belly of a whale and had just been regurgitated out. Soft snow was falling and clinging onto their hair and clothes. Many of the children sobbed in relief to be out in the light again; some remained very quiet, lost in their own world.

They brought the distraught children to the Guard station. They told their incredible story to the officer in charge, who was the same one Aunt Kay had spoken to the previous day.

"I can tell you what happened to the children. I don't know if you'd believe me, but I have never lied. You can ask my Mam that," said Mary. The officer nodded for her to proceed.

Mary did her best to relay her experiences, tumbling and hesitating through her words whenever something unusual came up, which, of course, were very frequent. But Mary looked the officer in the eye throughout and did not leave anything out. Mam and Aunt Kay encouraged her, agreeing and retelling their version of events as well.

After more than two hours, they had completed their statements. Tom became very restless and began to fidget and bounce on Mam's knees, eager to get away. The officer kept silent as he listened to the most remarkable statement he had ever heard in his career and carefully recorded every word.

At the end, he thanked them for their courage in rescuing many of the kidnapped children.

"Do you believe me?" said Mary.

"Yes," he said sadly. "I lost my niece to that monster."

***

Mary walked beside Mam, Tom sleeping quietly in her arms. Aunt Kay held her very last cigarette in between her first and middle fingers. They found themselves standing outside Saint Mary's Cathedral. Someone had actually built a snowman next to the bench they had sat on the other day. It stood a head taller than Mary, with black stones for eyes and a button for its nose.

"Here you go, mate, this ought to help keep you warm," said Aunt Kay, jabbing her cigarette into where the snowman's mouth ought to be.

They walked home in a daze. When they arrived at the apartment, Mam immediately ran a hot steaming bath, with loads of bubbly soap, for herself and Tom while Mary used the shower, their soiled clothes bound for the rubbish bin. They felt remarkably refreshed afterward, but it would take more than a lifetime of showers to cleanse the scars they had acquired in the Beastie's hall.

They found Aunt Kay, who had come up with them, lying prone on the couch, boots and all, already snoring while awaiting her turn to use the bathroom. Her thick hair covered the bloody patch where the raven had pulled out some of the strands.

Mary and Mam climbed into the bed, with Tom in the middle, and together fell into a deep, dreamless sleep.

CHAPTER 23
ONE OF US

"That's *it*, Ted! You lazy, good for nothing swine! I'm *definitely* leaving you today!

"If you want to leave, then *leave!!!* I'm sick and tired of hearing your whiny voice!"

Warm sunlight streamed through the window, casting a soft glow to the interior of the small, tidy apartment. Mary cracked open an eye, and the first thing she saw was Tom smiling down at her. He was sitting up next to her head, his round, pink face beaming brightly.

Mary held his right hand, circling the chubby palm with her thumb. "You're my *fave* thing."

To which Tom ran a spit-covered left hand all over her face. "And that, was definitely *not* my fave thing."

Mam was on the other side of the bed, also just woken up, listening in blissful contentment to the neighbors' bickering, the most beautiful sound she had ever heard.

A snoring from the couch reminded Mary that Aunt Kay was sleeping there. She recalled the events of the previous evening as if remembering a dream or nightmare, depending on how one viewed such things. Even now, they seemed so unreal, as if they belonged to a different ten-year-old girl.

"Sleep ok, girl?" asked Mam.

"Like a log."

"Hungry?"

"Oh yes! Starving!"

They jumped out of bed, Tom bouncing on his haunches. They devoured a hastily prepared breakfast of tea and toast, *crusty butts* and all, spread with sweet strawberry jam.

The sound of the kettle boiling and the smell of toast, managed to stir Aunt Kay, who stretched and yawned like a lion.

Toast in hand, Mary went to the window and opened it. This time, Mam let her stand there to enjoy the view. After last night, her little girl could just about handle anything.

Mam stood by her daughter's side. A pristine white seagull landed on the sill, a baby rat in its beak. It gave them an inquisitive look before taking off again. The sun was shining rather oddly, stronger than usual, with patches of blue sky visible amongst the white clouds. Bird song mingled with the brash cawing of seagulls and crows.

Three thin teenagers, wearing thick sports jackets, were standing on the pavement below, smoking foul-smelling cigarettes, arguing loudly about the merits of blindly supporting football clubs that do not even know they existed.

Mam gave the three young men a cheerful wave, calling out, "Nice weather we're having, eh, lads?"

They looked up at the two ladies, nothing except bewilderment in their eyes.

"Hello, unsavory people!" Aunt Kay came up suddenly beside them at the open window, giving the three teenagers a big grin. "You three look beautiful, you know that?!"

The teenagers promptly left.

"You should stop smoking!" shouted Aunt Kay to their backs. "They're bad for you!"

"Yeah! They cause *premature facial wrinkles!*" hollered Mary behind a cupped hand, and they all fell back laughing.

Mary wrinkled her nose. "Aunt Kay, shower, please!"

Knock…
Knock…
Knock…

"*AAAGGGHHH!*" The three screamed and jumped simultaneously at the loud knocking. Tom stopped sucking his big toe and blinked rapidly.

Knock! Knock!

"Hey, open up, it's me," came a familiar male voice with a sing-song accent.

Mary ran to open the door to find Èsa standing there, this time wearing jeans, a thick leather jacket, and a bobbled, blue-white woolly hat.

"The weather is just beautiful this morning. I thought I'd pay you guys a visit. Why was everybody screaming?" he said cheerfully, stepping in. "*Urgh!* Did something just die in here?" he said, covering his nose just as his eyes settled on Aunt Kay, who had the good grace to take a few steps back.

Èsa hurriedly took out a plastic packet from his carrier bag. "Here, I brought some dried mint leaves!"

"Yay!" said Mary, though she had never tasted mint before. She was just happy to have her friend there. Aunt Kay looked slightly less offended.

"I have something else," said Èsa, taking out a brown paper bag. "I'd just spent the past half hour talking to this nice old lady and her son downstairs. When she knew I was on the way up here, she gave me this and said it was a gift."

Mam shook out the contents onto her hand and inhaled the aroma deeply.

"What is it?" said Èsa.

"Ahh… yes, Lyon's tea," said Mam. "Now you're definitely one of us, mate, whether you like it or not!"

"Sorry?"

"Never mind," said Mam, smiling, glad for the distraction over the events of last night. "Please, have a seat. We're just having breakfast."

Èsa sensed some underlying tension in the room. "Umm, it's ok. I can come back some other time."

"No, don't be silly, you just got here," Mary grabbed Èsa's hand and dragged him to the table.

"You guys go ahead. I'll join you later," said Aunt Kay, stepping hurriedly into the bathroom to have a long, hot shower.

"Will I make us some mint tea?" offered Èsa.

"You just sit. I'll make it," said Mam, leaving the two sitting at the table.

While Mam was busy making the tea and preparing more toast, Mary turned to Èsa and asked quietly, "What was in that bottle you gave me?"

"That? It was pure Musk oil and lavender with just a hint of jasmine. My mother's favorite scent. Nice, isn't it?"

"Yeah, very nice. I, *ummm*, finished it all."

Èsa laughed good-naturedly. "Really? You should have given some to your aunt!"

Mary fished out the empty glass bottle from her pocket, cork-stopper back in place. Èsa looked in surprise, first at the bottle, then at Mary's serious face. Normally, just a tiny drop of the Musk oil would have been sufficient to last its user the whole day with its fragrance. If used infrequently, a full bottle would have lasted many months. There were no visible cracks on the bottle to indicate that the girl had inadvertently dropped it.

In that brief moment, the young man surmised something serious, very serious, had happened to this family and very recently as well. Everybody seemed on a knife edge, even with their welcoming nature and quick smiles. His sharp nose had also picked up a sharp metallic tang in the air, covered up by soap and other homely smells, but still definitely there. His suspicions were aroused earlier when he had noticed the red stain on Aunt Kay's collar the moment he stepped in the door. He chose to keep all these to himself for the moment.

"Not to worry. I'll get you another bottle."

Mam came at that moment carrying a plate piled high with warm toast and a steaming pot of extra strong, extra sweet tea to complement the mint she had added. Tom sat in his baby chair, a drool-drenched toast crushed in his hand. Aunt Kay joined them soon after, smelling as fresh as a daisy, her hair washed and cleverly combed to cover the injury.

After breakfast, everyone was in much better spirits. The good mood was further enhanced by the weather, which was getting sunnier by the hour.

"So, any plans Èsa?" asked Mam.

"To be honest, apart from coming here, I have no plans, really, though I wouldn't mind stretching my legs for a bit. I haven't had a good long walk in ages."

"Can I come?" asked Mary.

"Yeah, me too," said Aunt Kay. "I need some fresh air to clear my head since…." She glanced at Èsa, not wishing to talk about last night with someone they had only known recently.

If Èsa had noticed the awkward moment, he did not seem to mind. "Who knows, one of the barber shops might just be open. I'm desperate for a haircut!"

Mary looked up at his tall afro and giggled. "Yeah, you could hide anything in there!"

"Oh yeah? And what's this behind your ear?" Èsa placed his hand behind Mary's left ear and did a slow-motion grabbing motion. In a flourish, he opened his fist. Everyone gasped in astonishment at the small, stoppered glass bottle, which looked exactly like the one in Mary's pocket, filled to the brim with a dark, golden liquid.

Èsa looked hard at Mary then, a strange gleam in his eyes. "I told you once that if you ever needed me, I'll be there." The scents of lavender and jasmine suddenly filled the room. "Now, are you ready to tell me what happened last night?"

Thus, Mary, after getting nods from Mam and Aunt Kay, told Èsa everything.

Chapter 24
His True Name

Mary recounted the events of the past few weeks slowly, careful that she would not leave anything out. Mam and Aunt Kay remained silent, letting Mary tell the story unhindered. Although they had heard Mary's first encounters with the Beastie already, reliving the experience again through Mary's words was no less terrifying.

Mary told about the Beastie's visits, knocking on the door and granting her three wishes, and the enchantment he would cast over the rest of the family. She described in as much detail as possible the flour that Aunt Fay discovered at her flat, the missing neighbors, and the squished rats.

She recounted how the Beastie's appearance and size could change, seemingly at his discretion, and his insistence that she should grant him permission before crossing the threshold into their apartment.

Mary began to shake with uncontrolled emotions as she told Èsa how the previous evening, the Beastie had paid them a fourth visit, his manipulating her into giving up Tom and the desperate plight in search of his dark lair. Her eyes moistened with tears as she described what they saw in that place of horrors.

Mary related how the Beastie had reacted strongly to certain words or phrases, such as *keeping promises, minding his manners,* and most of all, *mother.*

At this juncture, Mary explained to Èsa how her own self had begun to change. She was initially unaware of the Beastie's visits, but she had begun to feel very anxious and fearful, although she could not understand the reasons. She was experiencing dark dreams and attacks of severe headaches.

"There was this wall I keep seeing, hurting my brain," Mary said. "But the wall cracked and was gone that night we slept at the mosque." Mary told everyone her dream of seeing these beautiful angelic beings lifting her wishes up to heaven. Since that night, Mary described developing a special sixth sense, being able to see things that others were blind to.

At this point, Èsa, who had been listening attentively in silence, inhaled sharply but still resisted the urge to disrupt the young girl's flow.

Tears flowed freely now down Mary's cheeks as she described how, after the game of riddles, she had been able to see into the Beastie's head through a giant wall of iron. She saw his past from centuries ago, although she was not sure how she knew this. She saw his true self and knew his true name.

"Tadgh…"

Mary had to stop several times in sorrow and anguish as she recounted the devastation visited on the young boy: his kidnapping, the heartbreaking loss of his mother, the dark times he spent being tormented in the coven's cave, his attempt to escape, and the black spell that brought the awful change in him.

"He went back home to find his mother," Mary sobbed uncontrollably. "Then he became angry and killed all the witches. He slept after that for a long time. I think he only wakes up whenever there's a very long winter."

Finally, Mary told of the sudden appearance of the black bird and the witch in the Beatie's lair. "He seemed to think she's the same one he had killed in that cave."

"And that ugly hag took my hair. Can you imagine an old, wrinkled crone with a head of hair like mine?!" Aunt Kay chipped in for the first time. Èsa glanced very briefly at Aunt Kay's mass of fizzy blonde hair but chose not to comment.

"They vanished into thin air, and we made it out of there this morning," said Mary softly. She dapped at her eyes with her sleeve. Both Mam and Aunt Kay looked very upset, eyes downcast.

"I splashed the perfume you gave me straight in his face," finished Mary. "I don't know why I did it, but...I just did... I think it helped, you know, somehow forced him to remember, to look past that iron wall in his brain..."

Mam said, "What do you make of all this, Èsa?"

Èsa looked thoughtful before replying, "*Hmmm...* first, I think it's time for that walk."

CHAPTER 25
A SPARKLING RAINBOW

"There she is, lads. The Monument of Light. The pride and joy of Dublin. Beautiful, isn't she?"

Mary, Mam, Aunt Kay, and Èsa (who was given the honor of carrying Tom, who, in turn, was trying to grab someone's cap) were standing at the base of the Spire, craning their necks up to see the very top. The sun was straight overhead, creating a circular sparkling rainbow at the pointy tip of the spike, quite dazzling to the eye.

"Yes, she certainly is," said Mary.

"One would imagine that if a giant was to accidentally sit on it…" said Èsa, wrestling ineffectively with Tom.

"Yes," agreed Aunt Kay. "We had actually quite recently contemplated that very point."

They crossed the road and walked down Henry Street, the sound of someone belting out *Raglan Road* on a six-string clear in the crisp morning air.

They came across a mime, the kind who only moved and petted your head if you placed some coins in his hat lying on the ground. They took a moment to watch as child after child came up shyly and gifted the mime some coins. Mary decided not to give the mime her only coin and instead handed it over to a tall, white-bearded man with a ponytail, who gave her a nod of thanks as he began the first notes to *Oh Danny Boy*.

"I was wrong," said Aunt Kay.

"Hmmm?" asked Mary.

"These street buskers, they're wonderful! If we could only find some hot, juicy kebabs, this day would be perfect!"

Mary could hardly believe this was the same street they had walked down just a couple weeks ago. Where before, this street, in fact, the whole of the city, was reeling under months of severe freezing weather; the shops closed, and the streets deserted.

This morning, literally overnight, the city had woken up from its long slumber. The snow drifts melted under a sun blazing down from a sky of the most beautiful blue. The gale force winds had trickled down to a cool breeze, almost as if the frost giants had finally begun to run out of breath.

The city's inhabitants began appearing outside their homes, tentatively at first, not daring to believe the snowstorm was actually coming to an end. Soon, the streets were filled with sounds of chatter and laughter as people from all walks of life thronged in larger groups, eager to rediscover their city from under all that ice and snow. Small children ran about with cheery faces, watched by worried parents as the streets and pathways became wet and slippery from the slush. The great hum and buzz of life spread rapidly, infecting everyone throughout the city and beyond.

As they walked towards the end of Henry Street and entered Parnell Street, Èsa began to explain what he thought had happened to Mary and her family.

"I didn't want to say anything in the apartment in case someone was listening. One can never be too careful where black magic is concerned." Èsa glanced at the Mam and Aunt Kay as he said this. "I believe everyone is on board that magic is at the heart of this?" Everyone nodded. "Not just your ordinary sleight of hand or minor illusion, but magic of the darkest variety, originating from ancient times."

"But why is all this happening now?" asked Aunt Kay.

"Magic has always been around, here in Ireland,

in Africa, in fact in every nation, since the first human civilization existed thousands of years ago. It's just hidden, secreted away from view, behind spiritual veils, barriers...or..."

"Walls," said Mary.

"Yes, and some of the strongest magicians can manipulate these walls, enhance their potency so that affected individuals could go through the most bizarre, most terrible experiences, yet never become aware of what was happening to them."

"Please bear with me," said Èsa as he saw the others struggling with the concept. "It's not something that is easy to explain, but if you could accept that there is this barrier between the spiritual realm and the physical, tangible world we live in, then we've made a good start."

They stopped walking and huddled closer together so as not to be overheard by the passers-by.

"For the *most* part, there is no interaction between the two worlds, each to their own, minding their own business. Sometimes, though, for reasons as simple as human greed and selfishness, the two worlds collide. What happened to that young boy so long ago, when those witches enacted their dark ritual, changing him, was one such example.

"Now comes the other interesting bit. Some

individuals have the ability, or develop this talent, to see through the veil to the other side at will. Call it intuition, sixth sense, a third eye, whatever. Many don't even realize they have it. They may be plagued by nightmares and visions and go through their whole lives suffering in silence, even end up labeled as crazy or something."

Èsa stopped to ensure everyone was following him. "I know this because I am one such individual. And what's more, I'm fairly certain you have this ability as well, Mary."

"You think…" began Mary.

"*Oh, thank God!*" cried Èsa suddenly. He handed Tom to Mam and ran off. The others were so surprised by the abrupt change they simply stood watching open-mouthed as the young man ran into a shop that was just opening its doors, with *Barber* marked on the window. Ten minutes later, he came out beaming, afro completely shaved, revealing a short stubble on his perfectly round head. "*Ahhh.* It's been a year since I've had a proper head shave. It feels *sooo* good!"

Without breaking stride, he took Tom back from Mam and continued. "We don't know why or how someone develops this ability. But I think you've got a strong dose of it, Mary, which is very rare over so short a period of time."

"Yeah, I sort of knew where to find them when he took Tom, and when I threw the perfume, suddenly I could see like... like a light breaking through the wall inside his head. It was pretty weird."

"Pretty *impressive,* I'd say! I don't think I'd developed mine to that level when I was your age."

They passed several oriental restaurants, the delicious aromas of cooked rice and stir-fried dishes wafting into the streets, making their mouths water.

"You must be wondering if I added anything to that perfume that I gave you?"

"Well, yes," said Mary.

"To be honest, nothing. Simply pure, distilled musk. Quite expensive, I must add, reserved in the old days only for royalty and the very rich and powerful. My family came from a long line of perfumists, you see."

All three ladies perked up their ears. They had not heard Èsa talk about this part of his family before.

"In Burkina Faso, our family was known as the *Attars* for many generations. Our ancestors journeyed from the Middle East, bringing the secret art of perfume distillation, and settled in Western Africa. The recipe and methods have been passed down from father to son over seven generations, by word of mouth only, with nothing ever written down. We ply our trade behind closely guarded doors, creating a few batches only every year, catering for the royalty and noble folk from all over Africa, the Middle East, and Asia."

"Wow!" said Aunt Kay. "You'd make a great salesman! So that tiny bottle of the stuff Mary threw at the beast, was it expensive?"

Èsa gave a small smile. "A couple of hundred euros."

"Ah, well, that's not too bad, then."

"…per mill…"

"Oh…"

"When I said nothing was added, that is true. It's so pure that even a tiny amount would fill up a reasonable sized room with its fragrance. Many of our people believe that these scents have healing properties, especially when people are afflicted by spiritual ailments, like the *evil eye* or black magic."

Mary drummed her fingers on her chin shrewdly and said, "I think I understand. If you have a good heart, you tend to like nice smells and give off a good aura. But if someone has real badness in them… I think I can actually *smell* this, like something rotten coming from the person."

Èsa looked at Mary with that strange light in his eyes. "Precisely. You are indeed gifted, little Mary."

"What happens now, Èsa? Are we free from this beast and that witch?" inquired Mam.

"In a way… yes, I don't think you'll have much trouble from either of them, at least for a while. Also… I'm still not certain, but from the way you guys described everything, I don't think the Beastie is the bad guy here…"

"Not bad?!" said Aunt Kay harshly. "After all he's done?"

"Please allow me to finish. We have something similar in Africa called Voodoo, a particularly vile form of black magic, where magicians use dolls to control or hurt others. People say they could reanimate corpses of animals, even humans, although, *thank God*, I've never seen one. I think the Beastie was used in a similar way, but I have to do more research on this."

They had just passed a restaurant which had a small alleyway running down its side for deliveries.

"Don't be alarmed, but it is very likely you'll get one more visit from him, not to do harm, but I think more a cry for help."

"How do you know all this?" asked Mam.

Èsa suddenly lowered his voice. "Keep walking. Don't make any sudden moves. I know this because he's been following us ever since we left your flat."

Mary felt a soft touch on her mind at that precise moment and saw movement in her peripheral vision. She sensed a small pale shadow crouching behind a rubbish bin as they walked past.

"Yes, I saw him," said Mary quietly.

"What?! Where?" whispered Aunt Kay, forcing herself not to look around.

"We already passed him, but I don't think you can see him. He was just a shadow, like a…like a living cartoon."

"What else did you see?" asked Mam as they picked up the pace, subconsciously going a different way to head back home.

"Nothing else, but he didn't smell as bad as last time."

CHAPTER 26
GOODBYE TADGH

Knock…
Knock…
Knock…

"You can't come in." Mary was standing on her stool, peering out the peephole. This time, Mam and Aunt Kay were fully aware, standing close behind Mary, Tom safely in Mam's arms.

The Beastie stood a few paces back from the door so Mary could see him. He still looked like a hideous hybrid of human, goat, and hog, with his short, curved horns, hog nose and chin, and scraggly beard. He was wearing a dark green three-piece suit, a dented bowler hat held in front of him in his furry paws.

As he peered back at Mary, she noticed something different about him, though. His eyes. They were no longer the dead, yellow eyes with the black horizontal pupils. Instead, staring back at her was a pair of normal green eyes, that of a scared, lonely boy.

"I'm sorry," Mary said. "But you're not allowed to come in."

"Darn right, you're not, Pork-face!" shouted Aunt Kay. "Or I'll shock the living daylights out of you!" She took out her taser gun.

"...*flashlight mode in operation...*"

" Blast this thing!"

"And I'll crush you with this." Mam hoisted up a brand-new rolling pin in her other hand, the *Minnie Mincer.*

"Please," said the Beastie in a boy's voice. "I don't need to come in if I'm not wanted. I just came to say I'm sorry...for...the pain...for everything."

"Fine! Run along now. Get away from here!" said Aunt Kay.

"Mam, Aunt, it's ok. Please let him finish. I don't think he means us any harm this time," said Mary.

They heard the sound of a boy sobbing from the other side. Eventually, it stopped, and his voice came again.

"Thank you. I also wanted to say goodbye. The winter is coming to an end. I should be back asleep by now, but something's different this time. I don't feel the extreme tiredness like I usually do," said the Beastie, rocking on the heels of his shiny black boots, not really sure what he was trying to say.

"Who cares?!" cried Aunt Kay.

"Aunt Kay, please!" This time, Mary looked at her aunt, a commanding tone in her voice.

"Ok, but make this quick, Luv. He's really giving me the creeps. What the heck does he want anyway?"

"Is there anything we can help you with?" asked Mary, her eyes back at the peephole.

"I don't know." The Beastie was looking down at his boots. "I don't really know why I'm even here, bothering you again. The world I see now is so different to the one I left behind. I don't remember much... but I feel I have done... things... many terrible things..."

"You don't remember?"

"I remember my old life, as a boy, with my Mam." His voice started to crack, and Mary could feel overpowering waves of sorrow permeating through the door. Her heart began to break all over again. "I remember being very angry at those witches for what they did. I... I... became so angry, I... I..."

"You're a killer, you nasty, horrid pig-man!" shrieked Aunt Kay.

This time, Mary turned and placed her hand on

her Aunt Kay's shoulder. She gently pushed her aunt back; a soft touch, but a gesture Mary had never done before. Aunt Kay looked taken aback but nodded for her to continue.

"I know what happened in the witches' cave," said Mary to the Beastie. "It wasn't your fault! They were the ones who hurt you and your Mam. They were going to sacrifice you. They used their awful magic to change you."

The Beastie wiped a tear with the back of a hairy paw. "The next thing I remember, was standing in that hall with this terrible headache, and then I saw you."

He gave a shudder. "Was that where I lived? Did I do all that?" He began to sob again with grief, putting his arms around himself while Mam placed a comforting hand on Mary's shoulder.

"We can't believe all he says," Mam whispered in Mary's ear. "Be careful, Luv."

Thereafter followed a silence from behind the door. Mary could not see any sign of him through the peephole. After a minute, they thought the Beastie had left. Then his head popped back into view.

"But I *do* remember that crone, though, who calls herself Glitter." An underlying threat entered his voice. "She was the one who killed my Mam. She did all of this to me. I think… I'm pretty sure she was with me when I slept in her cave. Hiding inside me… inside my head. I don't know how. I thought she was already dead."

Mary recalled suddenly the raven shadow that traveled up the Beastie's body when they were in his lair, soon after he had regained his memories when that wall broke surrounding his brain.

"The ritual the witches did to you made their magic very strong, enabling them to do really awful things. Maybe that's how she is still alive?"

"In my long slumber throughout the cold months, I kept dreaming of that black raven of hers. It was her pet, her familiar even; she kept feeding it bits of meat and small animals in her cave, and it would help her when she went hunting," said the Beastie.

Mary drummed her fingers on her chin shrewdly, the way she did when thinking very hard. "It's possible she used her familiar, that bird, as part of the magic to cheat death. Then, she used you, too. She got inside your brain and stole your memories. She controlled you to get to all those children. Controlled you like a doll in *Voodoo* magic!"

"I've tried to look for her. I've searched this whole city. Not a trace of her ugly face."

"Look who's talking," whispered Aunt Kay,

receiving a sharp nudge from Mam.

"But she can't hide from me forever. I've got powers of my own now. I'm no longer just a boy anymore. She knows I'm after her. There's nowhere to hide for that witch!"

"What if she went across the waters to some other place?" asked Mam all of a sudden.

"No, she can't, for the same reason I can't leave this island. Creatures like me, we're bound to this land. I'd simply die or fade away if I stepped off this island. I believe Glitter is the same. I suspect she's gone back to that cave if it's still there. No matter where she is, I'll find her. I'll make that witch pay!"

"Maybe revenge isn't such a good thing," said Mary. "Maybe you should focus on... you know... getting better? I have this friend who's really very..."

"Yes, I know all about your friend," The Beastie countered, getting angry again. "I don't like the look of him. I think he'd want to hurt me. He has the look of a hunter, that one."

"No, Èsa is so nice, and he knows a lot about this kind of stuff. He can help."

"No one can help me. I'm just a monster, a savage beast!" said the Beastie sadly. "The only thing left for me is to find my Mam's killer. What else can I do? And don't forget: Glitter's a black witch. She needs to do her own hunting to maintain her powers. More children would be taken by her. So, it's not just for my Mam. I'm doing this to make up for all the hurt I've caused. As long as I keep that witch busy, looking over shoulders, minding her back, then people should be safe from her."

Mary smiled from behind her peephole. "Then, I wish you well."

"I also can't bear the sight of that ridiculous blonde hair of hers. That needs a proper burning!"

Aunt Kay stuck out her tongue at the door.

The Beastie turned to go. On impulse, Mary said, "Wait! I promised you a gift the last time you were here, to remember me by if you were to go away. Just not my brother, of course!"

"*Mary!!*" hissed Aunt Kay.

"I'd like that," said the Beastie.

Mary pictured her gift clearly in her mind, then said, "I give to you my *other* favorite thing."

With that, the Beastie left, carrying the red apron tucked under his arm, with the words *Favorite Sister* etched on it.

"Is he gone?" asked Aunt Kay.

"Yeah, he's gone," said Mary softly, still facing the peephole, tears flowing again from her eyes.

"Will the Beastie ever come back?" asked Mam.

"No, I don't think he'll come knocking again, Mam."

"No," said Tom from Mam's arms, his second word.

Mary smiled down at her baby brother, her most favorite thing in the whole wide world. She then placed her forehead against the door, willing her thoughts to flow through the wood, down the streets of Dublin, towards the lonely figure receding into the distance, whose shadow was of a small, scrawny boy, filling her thoughts with warmth and friendship, praying they would reach him.

"You're no beast in my book. Goodbye, Tadhg."

The End.

Haji SM hails from Dublin, Ireland, where he lives with his family. He loves reading children's fantasy books, having devoured most of the works by Enid Blyton in his younger days and of Roald Dahl and the Spook's Apprentice series by Joseph Delaney in his not so younger days.

When not doing the 9 to 5 daily grind, he would preoccupy himself with staring at birds and cats, walking at a furious pace in parks, and imagining martial arts moves.

Printed in Great Britain
by Amazon